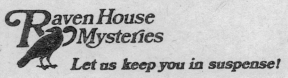

Antony Maitland had no premonition of danger

None at all as he started across the dark, quiet square toward his uncle's house. He reached the front steps and groped for his keys. Then the door swung open, leaving him silhouetted against the bright light from inside.

Suddenly the sharp crack of a shot echoed through the night. The tall, stately mirror in the hallway exploded into a thousand glittering splinters.

Maitland's would-be murderer had missed.

But would he next time?

THOUGH
I KNOW
SHE LIES

Sara Woods

A RAVEN HOUSE MYSTERY FROM
W🌐RLDWIDE
TORONTO · LONDON · NEW YORK

When my love swears that she is made of truth,
I do believe her, though I know she lies.

Shakespeare: *Sonnets*

Raven House edition published September 1980

First printing March 1980
Second printing September 1980

ISBN 0-373-60000-3

Prologue

THE PRISONER'S HAIR was red; the rich, dark shade so often described as titian, though the painter never lived who could capture its beauty fully. Now that the dusk was deepening outside, the lights in the courtroom came into their own, and it was as though the brightness of flame were tangled in it.

A tall woman ... that had been evident when first she came into the dock and stood for the indictment. It should have been possible to say she was simply dressed, but where was the simplicity in the perfectly cut suit she wore, in the nonsensical little cap—a spray of green leaves, no more—which must be regarded as sufficient deference to courtroom etiquette, but which hid nothing, detracted nothing from her beauty? Now she sat quietly, her hands clasped together in her lap; her expression was withdrawn, she might have been living in a world of her own instead of listening to the Solicitor-General, a sad-eyed, sad-voiced man, while he described to the court how she had murdered her sister. But in spite of her stillness there was not a man present, or woman either, who was not vividly aware of her.

Sir Nicholas Harding, Q.C., who led for the defense, was uneasily and rather angrily conscious of her impact on judge and jury; but his main attention was reserved for what his friend for the prosecution was saying. Beside him his junior, Derek Stringer, concentrated—eyes and thoughts alike—on the prisoner. He would have said, if asked, that he knew the prosecution's case by heart; a disingenuous defense against a possible charge of inattention, for he knew as well as anybody the importance that must be attached to its presentation. He certainly wouldn't have admitted that he didn't want to listen, didn't want to hear that calm, sad voice making point after point to the prisoner's discredit ... promising proof, proof positive of her guilt.

So he looked instead at the woman in the dock, and wondered

why—after all these years—he should have found, here, a woman who affected him in this way. It wasn't her looks, though her beauty was undoubted. When he considered only her appearance he could think of her almost dispassionately. What did a catalog of features amount to, after all? Her hair was thick, and shining, and drawn gently back from her face in an old-fashioned "bun"; a style which managed to be far more effective than the most elaborate coiffure designed by the most exclusive hairdresser. She had regular features, a creamy pale complexion, dark brows and lashes, and very expressive greeny hazel eyes. A generous mouth, he thought, she doesn't look like a poisoner, and of course she hasn't admitted . . . .

But there the evidence was, all neatly docketed, and now being displayed in gloomy tones by Sir Gerald Lamb for the prosecution. And no use pretending they were happy with the defense they had to offer, or that you could believe a thing just because you wanted to. If only he'd chosen to work some other circuit . . . never been called to the Bar at all . . . emigrated after the war . . . anything, in fact, rather than that he should be sitting here, fascinated, bewitched, appalled . . . watching her fate overtake her, and powerless to help.

1

JENNY MAITLAND HAD been painting the kitchen again, and when her husband got home unexpectedly early Friday evening he found newspapers all over the floor, and the last touches being put to one of the wooden chairs. Jenny sat back on her heels and eyed it critically.

"What do you think?" she asked.

An instinct of caution kept Antony in the doorway. "At least . . . it's unusual," he said. Walls and woodwork were inoffensive enough, but the color in which the chairs had blossomed might perhaps be held to justify the doubt in his tone.

"Cerise," said Jenny, swiveling the paint tin so that he could read the label in confirmation of her statement. "At least it's cheerful," she added defensively. "But, of course, if you don't like it I can start all over again." She waved the brush dangerously, as though indicating her willingness to change the color scheme of the entire room.

"Heaven forbid," said Antony, piously. "I don't want another week of makeshift meals."

Jenny looked up at him, and a gleam came into her eye. "If you weren't ashamed to be seen with me," she told him, "you'd take me out to dinner."

"If you can get the paint off your nose—"

"Paint or no paint," said Jenny firmly. She was wiping the surplus color off the brush onto a newspaper as she spoke, and Antony backed out of the room as she dropped the brush into the jar of turpentine and scrambled to her feet.

"I'd love to take you up on that," he said, regretfully. "But have you forgotten Mrs. Stokes is going out tonight?"

"And Uncle Nick's coming to supper. I haven't the faintest idea . . . do you think he'll mind an omelete?" She stepped gingerly across the paint pots, and pushed up the window over the sink; a stream of cold, damp air rushed into the warm room, mingling a whiff of fog with the previously undisputed smell of paint. "Is it dreadfully late?" she added. "I'll have to get this stuff off my hands before I can do anything."

"It's only half-past five."

"Then what are you doing here? I thought you were horribly busy with that awful little man who libeled somebody."

"We settled out of court. And not before time," Antony told her. "Otherwise that 'horrible little man' would find himself even poorer than he does at this moment. The only trouble is, Mallory's taken a huff; he wanted me to accept that brief from Watterson's, and I swore I wouldn't have time."

"Never mind," said Jenny. "There's always something. If you come in very carefully, Antony, you can open the cupboard door for me. But don't go near the chair."

"I won't." He followed her instructions with quite as much caution as she could have wished. "There's something to be said for Mallory's viewpoint, after all," he added, when he had retreated to the safety of the doorway again. "If I'd taken the brief from Watterson's, I could have afforded a new suit ... if I got paint on this one, for instance."

"There's no earthly need to get it all over you," said Jenny, rather spoiling the effect of this dignified pronouncement by pushing the hair back from her face and leaving yet another smear on her forehead.

"No need at all," her husband agreed solemnly. "But if you want the bathroom, love, I'll go down and use Uncle Nick's before he gets home. And don't say you'll only be a minute; a sweet disorder in the dress is all very well—"

He was grinning to himself as he went downstairs. Jenny in her more practical moments was always a joy, particularly as you never knew what she would turn her hand to next. This being a particularly dark and depressing November, perhaps cerise paint was only to be expected.

The house in Kempenfeldt Square (which belonged to Sir Nicholas Harding, that eminent and irascible Queen's Counsel) had been home to Antony for a great many years now. The upstairs flat which he and Jenny occupied had come into being as a temporary measure at the end of the war, and like many other temporary measures had imperceptibly achieved a state of permanence. It was a convenient arrangement, as Antony was in his uncle's chambers, and if Jenny ever got tired of legal shop she didn't say so. Probably she would have missed it now, just as Sir Nicholas would certainly have missed the convenient sanctuary of his nephew's quarters when his own household became too much for him. Mrs. Stokes, his housekeeper, was an amiable soul, but an expert in getting her own way; while as for Gibbs, who had been butler to Sir Nicholas's father, he ought to have retired years ago, but quite simply enjoyed being a martyr.

Dinner, luckily, was by no means as sketchy as might have been expected from Jenny's forboding tone. She had managed, moreover, to remove most of the paint, and by the time they were gathered round the fire with their coffee her brown curls were clinging to her head less damply, and the flush induced by over-enthusiastic scrubbing had subsided. Sir Nicholas, enjoying his after-dinner cigar, was looking unusually mellow, a circumstance which caused Antony to indulge in a brief examination of conscience. But for once, it seemed, there was no storm to follow this period of calm. His uncle even went so far as to commiserate with him on old Mr. Mallory's unreasonable behavior. "But if you've no immediate commitments," he added, "I might have a suggestion to make."

This was an unusually devious approach, and perhaps Antony might be forgiven for treating it with caution. "Something I can do for you, sir?" he asked, warily.

"I'm worried about this Canning affair," said Sir Nicholas, abandoning circumlocution for a bluntness that was much more characteristic.

Antony, who had been too busy until five that afternoon to bother with any list but his own, gave him a blank look, and Jenny prompted hastily: "The murder trial ... Barbara something-or-other. It started today."

"Oh, that one," said Antony, enlightened. "I thought it was quite straightforward, sir. Nothing out of the way."

"That is not altogether correct. For one thing the prisoner— Barbara Wentworth, my dear—" he put in for Jenny's benefit, "is a very unusual woman. I might almost say ... stunning," said Sir Nicholas, with a sidelong look to gauge his nephew's reaction. "I use the word advisedly," he pointed out, and smiled grimly at Antony's startled look.

"I see." He sounded doubtful.

"A gorgeous creature," Sir Nicholas went on with enthusiasm. "One of the most beautiful women—"

"If she's such a smasher," Antony interrupted crudely, "I don't quite see what you're making a fuss about."

"You feel I should be content with an ascetic enjoyment of the picture she presents?" said his uncle. "You may have a point there, but unfortunately I have also my junior to consider."

"Derek?"

"If I say he has fallen in love I shall not be conveying my meaning, so I find myself compelled to resort to your own phraseology; my learned friend, Mr. Stringer, has gone off the deep end over our client," said Sir Nicholas with an air of distaste.

"Oh," said Antony. And was unwise enough to grin.

"There is nothing funny in the situation. If you think—"

"But, sir, *Derek!*"

"It can't be serious, Uncle Nick," said Jenny. "Derek never is."

"You think not? I admit, my child, I am unskilled in these mysteries, but I know when a man is making a fool of himself," said Sir Nicholas, bitterly.

"Well, granted that, sir ... what can I do about it?"

"Perhaps my request is not directly connected with the statement I have just made." Antony grinned to himself at the judicious tone; he knew very well that the gambit had been chosen deliberately to rouse his interest ... it was the way he would have played the hand himself. "But I feel there is room for some further investigation. I am not at all easy in my mind, and Bellerby agrees with me—"

"Bellerby is her solicitor, is he?"

"Yes. He told me from the beginning that the matter called for your 'special talents'; you may recall, he has used that phrase before?"

"Delicately put," said Antony, with appreciation, "when all he means is my infernal curiosity." He got up as he spoke, to put a piece of coal on the fire, and stood for a moment watching the results of his handiwork as the flames leaped hungrily around it. Then he turned and looked down at his uncle. "Let me understand you, sir. You're inviting me to meddle?"

"I'm asking your help. In the circumstances, 'meddle' is hardly the word I should have chosen."

"Isn't it, sir?" Antony's tone was dry. "You've used it so often to describe my activities—"

Sir Nicholas smiled at him. "I'm glad to know my comments don't got altogether unheeded," he remarked, affably. "But I won't quarrel with your phraseology . . . I'm *asking* you to interfere."

"At this stage, Uncle Nick? With the trial already started?"

"Do you imagine I should make such a request," said Sir Nicholas, frostily, "if I were not impelled by a strong sense of urgency?"

"No, of course. But what do you think I can do?"

"Probably nothing. I'm only asking you to try. And at this stage," he added, "I just want you to listen."

"Well . . . all right." He still sounded hesitant, but he knew as he spoke that he was committing himself . . . not just to hear the story; and his gesture conveyed, accurately enough, the surrender of his position. "All I know is, this girl—"

"Barbara Wentworth."

"—is accused of poisoning her sister. Did she do it?"

"There is a strong circumstantial case. She is pleading 'Not Guilty,' and I find no great difficulty in accepting her word, though I wouldn't say I was convinced she is telling the truth."

"But Derek thinks she is?"

"Nothing so reasonable," said Sir Nicholas. If he was gratified to have obtained his nephew's attention, he gave no sign. "He doesn't admit it, but he's fully convinced of her guilt. Ever since Bellerby took us to see her . . . do you think he has Puritan ancestry?"

"He doesn't behave as if he had," said Antony, carefully. And, indeed, Derek Stringer, a friend of long standing, was as cheerful a bachelor as he knew. "But I don't quite see—"

"I'd better give you the facts," said Sir Nicholas, neatly sidestepping an explanation of his train of thought. Jenny got up and collected his coffee cup and refilled it, and sat down again on the sofa. Antony went back to his chair.

"Expound," he said.

"I'll be brief," his uncle promised. "Barbara Wentworth had an older sister, Laura, who married—thirteen or fourteen years ago—a man called Douglas Canning. They were divorced three years ago, and the daughter, Clare, remained with her mother. They lived at Roehampton—the top flat in an old house which has been divided. In September last Laura fell ill, with a bad attack of influenza; Barbara went to stay with them, to help nurse her, though that is perhaps to exaggerate what was required. A Mrs.

Paley, in Laura's employ as a cleaning woman, looked after her during the day."

"Where does Barbara live?"

"She works in Knightsbridge, at a dress shop called Raymonde's," Sir Nicholas told him, "and shares an apartment with two other girls close by."

"What is she like?" asked Jenny.

Sir Nicholas divided a rather acid smile between them. "I gather she is a model, who also understudies for the manageress upon occasion. As for her appearance ... I told you, she's a beauty. And can you imagine," he added, obviously with a strong sense of grievance, "how much more difficult that makes it? I could hardly insist on an all-male jury—"

"Women aren't *all* cats," said Jenny.

"No, but ... you know what I mean," he appealed to his nephew. "An attractive girl, accused of murder—"

"Did you ask her to tone it down a bit?"

"Of course I did! She has red hair—did I tell you?—and her disposition is not really tractable. She said it would be just as much a lie as going into the witness box and swearing to something that wasn't true. I even had trouble to persuade her she couldn't appear in court without a hat."

"That should have helped matters. Didn't it?"

"If anything, it made them worse. What I had in mind," said learned counsel crossly, "was something in the nature of a candle extinguisher. Instead she turned up in a cap sort of affair, which seemed rather to highlight her hair than to hide it. Green leaves, or something," he added, glaring at Jenny as though she were somehow responsible for this unreasonable behavior.

"I expect it gives her confidence," she told him. "I don't think you can blame her for that."

"Blame her? I don't blame her. I just think she's as stubborn as a mule," said Sir Nicholas. "And between the two of you, you've quite destroyed the continuity of my narrative."

"You'd got to the point—I think—where Laura Canning was about to become deceased," said Antony, helpfully.

"In mid-September she was still in bed, but well on the way to recovery. I don't need to go into details, because the way she died isn't in dispute; she took an overdose of a sedative the doctor had prescribed ... one of the synthetic analgesics."

"That sounds more like suicide. Why do they think Barbara was responsible?"

"The medicine bottle was in the bedroom, no difficulty there; Laura could easily have poured it out for herself and left the bottle on the bedside table where it was found. But the glass had been taken away to the kitchen and rinsed carefully, and dried and put away. She could have done that, too, but it seems very unlikely. I told you it was an old house, converted into flats. The kitchen is a good way from the bedroom, at the end of a long, rather chilly corridor; there seems no reason why she should have gone to the trouble. But the really telling thing is that there's not a fingerprint of hers in the kitchen anywhere—she'd been in bed for a fortnight, remember, and presumably Mrs. Paley performs her duties conscientiously. And one can hardly visualize a woman whose last act in this world, after arranging as comfortable a death as possible for herself, is to put on a pair of gloves and go and do a little washing up."

"Quite unreasonable," said Jenny positively. "But if someone killed her, why did it have to be Barbara?"

"I said the case was circumstantial. She had been in the habit of giving her sister the sedative each night; and her fingerprints, and hers alone, were on the bottle. Even if she admitted she'd taken the glass away to wash, it would sound better. But she says when she got in at about ten-fifteen Laura already seemed drowsy and told her she'd had her medicine. And it never occurred to her to wonder why the glass wasn't on the bedside table."

"I see. And the motive alleged—?"

"I'm afraid here the case for the prosecution is almost overwhelming," said Sir Nicholas. "There is a long-standing source of grievance between the sisters in the disposition of their father's estate; there have admittedly been disagreements between them . . . you could hardly say they were on affectionate terms. And, more recently, a male acquaintance has been a cause of jealousy and dissension."

"The father's estate . . . Laura got the lot?"

"She was the elder by five years. Thirty-three years old at the time of her death," Sir Nicholas reminded him.

"All the same—"

"I'm afraid Lamb is prepared to go into all these matters at length," said Sir Nicholas sadly.

"Lamb? Yes, I suppose he would get it." Antony sounded thoughtful.

"He's leading Burns. A formidable team," his uncle pointed out. "Especially as I am not finding Stringer's attitude helpful."

"I should have thought, if he's really fallen in love with the girl—"

"He is terrified of every point that might be made in her favor, because he is sure there must be a catch in it somewhere, and that it will recoil on our own heads." Sir Nicholas ignored the doubt implied by his nephew's choice of words and spoke with less than his usual lucidity.

"Poor Derek," said Jenny. Sir Nicholas raised his eyes silently to heaven.

Antony, tactfully concealing his amusement, asked soberly, "What is the defense?"

"I've no choice but to try to suggest suicide in spite of all the indications to the contrary, of which I am as well aware as anybody."

"And what's to be my part in all this?"

"Go through my notes tonight and the rest of the material as soon as you can. There may be people you feel you could profitably see, even though Bellerby has been over the ground already. It's always possible, if the right questions had been asked in the first place, that there might be something helpful."

"Needle in a haystack, sir. Don't you think?"

"Of course I think so! Not being quite demented," said Sir Nicholas. "But will you look for it?"

Antony made no direct reply. "Do you really think she's innocent, Uncle Nick?"

"I've told you, I'm willing to believe it." He paused and then went on without any more prompting than his nephew's raised eyebrow supplied. "I admit, I like the girl. She has spirit, and a good deal of charm . . . which perhaps is more to the point. I've an uncomfortable feeling that what you uncover will only tend to strengthen the motive . . . which may be strong enough to convict her already. But I think we should try."

"Very well. And the trial started today," he added, in a considering way. He allowed his smile to broaden as Sir Nicholas grinned back at him.

"I've known you embark on more hopeless quests," he said.

"Today's Friday; we've had Lamb's opening address, and the police outline of the case ... more or less what I told you."

"Did anything emerge?"

The older man shook his head. "There was nothing we could profitably dispute, so we held our fire. When we get to the doctors—" He finished his sentence with a gesture, which his nephew had no difficulty in interpreting.

"There are two things that occur to me immediately," he said. "If someone gave Laura the medicine, wouldn't she notice she was taking too much?"

"I shall use that, of course, as an additional argument for suicide, but I'm afraid the answer is, she wouldn't necessarily have noticed. The stuff was almost colorless and tasteless, the doctor says; she took it in water, well diluted, and there was also a water jug to hand on the bedside table. The kind of person who mixed it had only to put more medicine, less water ... the exact amount required will have to be gone into in court, of course, but, frankly, I'm not expecting much help there."

"No, I see. Well, the other thing is Laura's will, if she made one."

"Did she leave anything to Barbara, you mean? I'm afraid she did."

"How much?"

"Five thousand pounds. The will was made after her divorce, and the residue goes to her daughter. Did I make it clear that Laura Canning was a wealthy woman?"

"How very depressing. There's nothing quite so understandable as a financial motive," said Antony, dispirited.

"And I suppose it means you'll be busy all the weekend," said Jenny. "I hate you, Uncle Nick."

"I took the liberty," said Sir Nicholas, ignoring her, "of asking Bellerby if he would see you in the morning, Antony. If he can take you to see Miss Wentworth, I think you may find that ... interesting."

"I'm sure I shall, sir." His tone was deceptively mild, and Sir Nicholas threw back his head and laughed.

"I've no doubt you're wishing me in Jericho," he said, "but I must say, I find a certain amusement in the situation."

"Yes, I know, sir. It's not without its irony." He got up and started to move across the room to the cupboard in the corner. "I think we'd better finish the brandy, Uncle Nick. I was saving it for a rainy day, but no doubt I could brave Gibbs's displeasure and raid your supply, in an emergency."

"Would it be the first time?" Sir Nicholas inquired, in a resigned tone. But he did not go so far as to refuse the offer.

"BUT WHAT DID HE MEAN," asked Jenny, carrying the glasses out to the kitchen after Sir Nicholas had gone, "by saying the situation was amusing? I don't see that at all."

"Reversal of roles," said Antony, following her. "Usually I'm trying to interest him in something, and he's resisting like mad."

"Oh, I see. I shall *not* wash these up tonight," said Jenny, but she turned on the tap to run water into the glasses. "Isn't it queer," she added, "that something like rinsing out a cup might come to mean so much?"

"Very queer," he agreed.

"Well, if she's innocent," said Jenny, "it must be terrible to be tried for murder."

"You might say, it would be worse if she was guilty. Or would it? But there's no telling, either way."

Jenny turned from the sink and reached for the towel to dry her hands. "It's funny about Derek, isn't it?"

"Do you think Uncle Nick's right about that? It doesn't seem very likely. I mean . . . love at first sight!"

"People do," said Jenny. "Sometimes. And . . . well, you know, I despaired of Derek ages ago—"

"I know you said you did."

"—but all the same, I think it might be true. Like the man in the song, you know. "

"I don't know," said Antony, patiently.

"The one who was always falling in love quite madly," said Jenny, as though that explained everything. "But I wish," she added with a sigh, "it hadn't been someone like this."

Antony put an arm round her shoulders and began to urge her out of the room. "Don't take it too much to heart, love," he advised. "It's probably nothing but indigestion."

"Even Uncle Nick," said Jenny, "couldn't mistake indigestion for love. But at least," she added, more cheerfully, "so far as you're concerned, it's just an ordinary case."

And, in its way, that was true . . . .

2

THE SMELL OF a woman's prison is unmistakably different from anything else in the world and was enough in itself to induce in Antony Maitland a strong sense of depression and of the hopelessness of human endeavor. He followed the solicitor, Mr. Bellerby, down a cheerless corridor and attempted to divert himself by wondering what Barbara Wentworth was really like. But his spirits were so low that the bare room into which they were presently ushered could depress them no further. He stood by the dusty window, which looked out only onto an air shaft, and waited for the prisoner to appear.

And inevitably he found that his expectations had misled him. The newspaper pictures, which he had studied more carefully last night, gave no idea of her quality; and from his uncle's description he had been expecting—unreasonably, perhaps—an attraction far more blatant. She came in quietly, her movements unstudiedly graceful; and the stumpy figure of the wardress who stood for a moment in the doorway before retiring and shutting herself outside could not have been—even by design—a more effective contrast. It was difficult to see a basis for Sir Nicholas's complaint: dress and manner were alike unassuming, and she could hardly be expected to dye her hair. And even if she had, he suspected it would make little difference; she was definitely not a woman you could ignore.

In these surroundings, Mr. Bellerby's normal cheerfulness was subdued. He made the introductions fussily and explained his colleague's presence—Antony felt—at too great a length. "You may remember, my dear, that I mentioned Mr. Maitland to you when first the question of your defense arose. Unfortunately, at that time, it did not seem that his commitments would allow him—"

So far, her attention had been all for her solicitor. Now she smiled at him gratefully and turned on his companion a long, considering look. He was holding his interest in the situation politely in check, she thought; and he looked younger than she had expected from what Mr. Bellerby had told her. A dark man with a thin, intelligent face ... a casual manner ... and something behind the casualness. "But I don't quite understand," she said, "how another lawyer can help me."

"There's no question of my accepting a brief at this stage, Miss Wentworth. But Sir Nicholas felt there were a few points that might usefully be cleared up."

Her eyes were no more than an inch below his own. She met his look steadily, but there was no reading her expression. After a moment, "I've told them everything I know," she protested. "Mr. Bellerby, and Sir Nicholas, and Mr. Stringer."

"Then you won't mind telling me again." They eyed each other gravely for a moment, and then he smiled and added persuasively, "I don't want to have to admit to my uncle that you threw me out."

Surprisingly, she laughed at that and sounded really amused. "In the circumstances, it would be churlish of me," she agreed.

"Not really. I can understand your reluctance—" There was something wary in her look, he thought, something not quite candid. But could she be completely natural when so much was at stake?

"We'd better sit down." She took a chair by the long table, and Mr. Bellerby followed her example; Antony remained standing by the window and looked down at her with more open curiosity now.

"I wasn't in court yesterday," he said, and saw her hands clench before she relaxed them deliberately, and raised his eyes to her face again to find it expressionless.

"But you know what they say. What the police say, and ... and—"

"I know the outline of the case for the Crown," he agreed. "My concern is to know how we can answer it."

Something in his tone seemed to sting her, so that she said swiftly: "Not how we can prove my innocence? Isn't it the same thing?"

"For the purpose of our discussion ... yes."

"I don't—"

"Our instructions are—from Mr. Bellerby here—that you are

not guilty," Antony told her. "You don't have to convince me . . . just the jury."

"All right! What do you want to know?" She was angry now, but she did not meet his eyes. Momentarily forgotten by both his companions, Mr. Bellerby murmured his agitated deprecation of these tactics.

"Start with the facts . . . the night your sister died. You went out, didn't you?"

"Yes, she was better really, there wasn't any need—"

"What time did you go?" He interrupted without ceremony, and saw her lips tighten. Angry, she was even more handsome, he thought with appreciation, than when her face was tranquil.

"Soon after eight o'clock. Brenda was there—Mrs. Mills's niece."

"Mrs. Mills—?"

"Laura's landlady. She lives in the downstairs flat. Brenda stayed until about nine o'clock, when Clare went to bed. I got back at ten-fifteen."

"Exactly?"

"No, not exactly. The police tried to make me fix a time, but it doesn't really seem very important."

"Don't you think so?" His tone was dry. "When did you first notice a clock, after you got in?"

She paused so long that he thought she wasn't going to answer. "I . . . don't remember," she said at last. The green eyes were fixed on him thoughtfully. "Why are you trying to make me angry, Mr. Maitland?" she asked.

He hadn't expected so much directness. "Have you heard the phrase *in vino veritas*, Miss Wentworth? Indignation sometimes works even better."

"You mean, I might answer without thinking?"

"Precisely. And as, unfortunately, I can't take you out on a pub crawl—" He heard Mr. Bellerby raise his voice in scandalized, though unintelligible, protest; but he kept his eyes on Barbara Wentworth's face and smiled at her, suddenly, disarmingly.

"You said you weren't interested," she pointed out, "if I was guilty or not."

"I said nothing of the kind . . . forgive me! I said that what *I* think doesn't matter."

"I see." Her eyes were dancing now, and her mouth quivered on the edge of a smile. "I'm sorry if I've spoiled your experiment."

"Think nothing of it. But are you going to tell me—?"

"Oh, yes, of course . . . that night. I didn't notice the exact time I got in. I went straight to Laura's room. She told me she'd already had her medicine—the sleeping stuff—and she seemed sleepy, so I just . . . straightened the bed . . . and went away."

"This must be distressing. I'm sorry."

"I'd be a fool to mind, wouldn't I?" she said, bitterly, "when you're trying to help me."

"Then tell me about the room. Was it as you'd left it?"

"Yes." she frowned a little over the question. "Yes, of course."

"No sign of Brenda Mills's visit?"

"Oh, I see. Well, she had pulled the easy chair a little nearer the bed; but she said Laura wanted to go to sleep, and that's why she didn't stay."

"Your sister was drowsy as early as nine o'clock?"

"I shouldn't think so. She didn't like Brenda, that would be just an excuse."

"So the chair had been moved. Had Laura been reading, do you think?"

"She had some magazines. One had fallen on the floor."

"Her slippers? Her dressing gown?"

"Her slippers were by the bed. Her dressing gown . . . oh, dear, *that* doesn't help, Mr. Maitland." She gave him a look that was almost comically rueful.

"Why not?"

"It was still in the cupboard. Brenda said Laura wasn't out of bed while she was in the flat, and if she'd worn it afterward she wouldn't have put it away."

So she understood the arguments against suicide only too well. "She wouldn't have gone to the kitchen without it?" he asked.

"No, I'm sure. Not that I think she would have done anyway. Why should she?"

"I wish I knew. But wouldn't she have gone to the bathroom before taking her medicine and settling down for the night?"

"That's just next door. It's quite a luxurious flat, Mr. Maitland. She had her own bathroom and wouldn't need to go out into the corridor at all."

"Then—" but this had obviously been thought of "—couldn't she have washed the glass without going to the kitchen?"

"But there wasn't a glass in the bathroom, not of any kind. And the one I'd left on the bedside table was back in the kitchen—clean—next morning."

"One tumbler is very like another." He was wondering as he spoke if anyone had looked in the garden, below the window. Perhaps she divined his thought; at any rate she shook her head at him.

"This wasn't a tumbler. Just a small, fancy thing with violets painted on it."

"And you didn't notice it wasn't on the table any longer?"

"No, I didn't."

"Nor look at the bottle."

"Well ... not to *see* it. I mean, if I had, I'd have seen it was nearly empty. And she only got it the day before."

"Was she taking any other medicine?"

"Only some tablets, one night and morning. There were just the right number left, and they weren't a sedative, anyway. Before that she had some red stuff, too—four times a day, after meals and don't forget to shake the bottle; but she finished it, and the doctor said she didn't need any more. The sleeping stuff she always took."

"Always?"

"Perhaps not, when she was well. But it was a regular prescription, and while she was ill the doctor said she should take it every night."

"I see. Anything else about the room?"

"Nothing else. I went to see if Clare was asleep, and pushed open the door a little, not letting the light disturb her. I could hear her breathing, regularly and very deeply, and so I came away."

"And then?"

"I went to bed."

"Did you go to the kitchen at all?"

"No. I'd washed up the supper things earlier, and anything else could wait for Mrs. Paley in the morning."

"Did you sleep?"

"Not at first. I was ... I was thinking about things. And I didn't hear anything during the night," she added, without waiting for the further question.

"What were you thinking about?"

"I don't know, really. Life ... I suppose."

He did not speak for a moment but let the silence lengthen. Barbara lookd down at her hands and then raised her eyes to his face again, but she did not attempt to amplify her statement, nor did the silence seem to shake her composure. After a while he looked away, out of the window at the brick-lined wall of the air shaft. "Where did you go that night?" he asked, abruptly.

"To meet a friend." As he turned quickly to look at her again, he found her eyes steady and a disconcerting little smile on her lips. No use to try any tricks, then; she saw through them only too easily. Which was a pity, because he realized suddenly that he wanted almost desperately to know the answer to one question . . . whether she was guilty as charged. And he had a nasty feeling it wasn't going to be all that easy to find out.

"Remember, all this is new to me." He returned her smile without any sign of resentment. "You can tell me—can't you?— at least as much as you've told the police."

"I suppose I can."

"Well, then. This friend—?"

"Stanley Prior. He had his car, and we drive to Richmond. There's a pub there, the Unicorn; it's busy in the summer but quiet once the season is over. We sat and talked, and then he drove me home. I mean, to my sister's, not my own place, of course."

"He didn't come in or stay talking for a while?"

"No, he drove straight off. It isn't really a good place to park." This was obviously an afterthought; he had the impression she was watching him now, to see how he took the statement.

"This was at ten-fifteen?"

"Somewhere around then."

"And what had you been talking about, you and Mr. Prior?"

"He told me he was going to ask Laura to marry him." There was just the faintest edge of defiance to her tone. Did she care? Or was she just afraid that somebody might think she did?

"Were you surprised?"

"Not at all."

Somehow he must make her amplify these rather flat statements. "He could hardly be asking your consent," he mused. "Did he want you to tell him how you thought Laura felt about him?" He proffered the suggestion cautiously and was disconcerted when she began to laugh.

"If you knew Stanley! No, he was in no doubt of his reception." She stopped, and seemed to be considering the remark, and added seriously: "To do him justice, I think he was quite right."

"You haven't told me why he went to such pains to confide in you." All trace of laughter had left her eyes now, and when she did not immediately reply he went on carefully, feeling his way. "You implied, I think, that he is—shall we say?—conceited. Was he, perhaps, breaking the news to you ... gently?" And this time, when he no longer wished to anger her, he succeeded only too well.

She gave him a fiery look, banged both fists down hard on the table, and said, "Damn you!" viciously. Mr. Bellerby clucked distressfully; he had rather the air of a nursemaid whose charges were both bent on disgracing him, but neither of them paid him the least attention.

"Just as you like," said Antony, equably. "I'm not asking what you felt, you know. Only what—in his conceit—he thought."

"Does it matter?"

"Of course it matters! He's being called by the prosecution."

She struggled with that for a moment and then said more calmly, "You won't believe me when I tell you I was quite indifferent about it; but you say it doesn't matter ... what *you* think of me. I'm quite sure *he* thought I should be upset. I've known him a long time; in fact, I introduced him to Laura."

"Does my uncle ... does Sir Nicholas know about this?"

"I didn't tell him. Of course I didn't tell him." She paused and then added, almost diffidently, "I suppose you mean they'll use it to prove motive?"

"I'm afraid they will." He came and sat down at the table and added quietly, "It's annoying, of course, but a very small thing compared with being tried for murder."

"Do you think so?" Now that he had moved, she turned her eyes to the window. "To me it seems ... the final humiliation," she said, and flushed as she spoke.

"You say you think your sister would have married him?"

"Oh, yes. He's an amusing companion, and very good-looking."

"Is that enough?"

She turned her head to look directly at him. "She didn't want someone to love," she said. "Just someone to possess." Her voice was flat and weary; and he wished, uncomfortably, that she was still sustained by the anger that had shaken her a few moments before.

"You weren't very fond of your sister?" he asked gently.

"No . . . n-no." And again, incredibly, the smile quivered. "I know they'll say I was jealous of her, but that isn't true. And I wished her well, even though I didn't like her, but nobody will believe that. When your memories go back to the nursery, it's . . . there's always a bond."

"I suppose so. Do you think she might have killed herself?"

"I didn't, of course. I wouldn't have gone out and left her alone with Clare."

"You could hardly stay with her indefinitely," he pointed out. "But I didn't mean that night particularly; I meant, did she have suicidal tendencies?"

That seemed to need some thinking out. "She was neurotic," she said at last. "But as for the other . . . I honestly don't think so."

"Had she ever threatened to take her own life?"

"Not to me." He opened his mouth to put a further question, but she went on without prompting. "Douglas told me she'd said it once to him, but we neither of us thought she meant it. I mean, if she had meant it she wouldn't have talked about it, would she?"

"Douglas . . . is that her husband?"

"Douglas Canning. Yes."

"Tell me about her marriage."

"What is there to tell? She was married when she was twenty and divorced three years ago. Clare is nearly twelve."

"I think," said Antony, amused, "you might find something more to tell me, if you really tried. The bare facts are all very well—"

"But I don't know any more. How can I know?"

"I'm not asking for a detailed analysis. Just how things looked, from your point of view. For instance, were you still living in Southbourne when the marriage took place?"

"Yes."

"Did Laura stay there after she was married?"

"No, they came to London. Douglas works for the Imperial Insurance Company."

"And you stayed in Southbourne with your parents?"

"Yes, for three more years. I came to town when I was eighteen."

"To seek your fortune?" And just as he was beginning to despair of anything but the barest facts, something—his light tone, perhaps—seemed to touch a responsive chord.

"To work in a dress shop," she said, and smiled as she spoke. "Not quite the same thing. You see, my parents didn't approve of my leaving home, but that was something I could do without training. And then I was lucky; one of the models made up her mind *that* was what I should be doing. And she taught me everything . . . how to walk, and that's not as easy as it sounds . . . how to turn round so as to show what you're wearing to the best advantage, and from all angles . . . how to slip out of a coat, and put it on again gracefully. And how to *act* in all the different kinds of clothes you have to wear. She was terribly kind. And she taught me, too, a lot of things a girl doesn't know when she's been at school all her life, and then just at home." She was telling him all this eagerly, as though it was important that he should understand; then she stopped and laughed a little self-consciously and added, "I don't think I realized till later, though, how much she'd done for me."

"So then you were ready for a different sort of job?"

"Oh, yes. I went to another firm, one of the big stores, and the money was better, but it was rather dull. And then my parents died . . . you must know this bit. My mother first, and my father a year later. He left everything to Laura. Everything except a hundred pounds."

"Why was that, do you think?" This didn't seem to come into the category of forbidden subjects. "A measure of his disapproval?"

"It didn't matter, you know. I didn't mind looking after myself. And the hundred pounds was useful."

Her tone was at once amused and defiant, so that Antony smiled and asked her, "What did you do with it?" leaving unanswered the question of motive which he had raised.

"I spent it on clothes. It took some doing, but I looked everywhere until I got a coat that was absolutely right, and all the right accessories. Window dressing, you know. And then I went to see Raymonde."

"That's the shop you're with now?"

"Yes. You see, madame wanted someone to help her with everything . . . all sides of the business. That's what I like about a small place, it's so much more fun. And, of course, the people who come in . . . but you don't want to hear about them."

It occurred to him that the recital might well be amusing, but he could hardly justify to himself a request for it—still less to Mr. Bellerby. "So your investment was a good one," he said.

"Very good."

"And after you came to town did you see much of your sister?"

"I . . . well, not a great deal. She used to like to know what I was doing; she didn't approve of the modeling any more than my parents did. But lately, the shop seemed to interest her, she used to come in quite often." She didn't sound as though the fact gave her much pleasure.

"But you still had nothing in common?"

"Nothing at all. Only . . . there was Clare."

"Are you very fond of your niece?"

"Fond . . . oh, yes. But . . . worried about her, too." She was looking full at him now and talking easily; and when she paused he had the feeling that she was challenging him in some way . . . challenging him, perhaps to understand what she was saying. "Given time," she said, "Laura would have devoured her."

"I see." He drew out the words, and suddenly she was speaking quickly, vehemently.

"You don't see. You don't believe me. I don't know why I'm telling you all this . . . when you don't believe me."

He made no attempt to reassure her, just waited a moment and then said quietly, "What was the cause of the divorce?" She hesitated, and he added in a bracing, impersonal tone, "Come now, Miss Wentworth, this a matter of fact. You won't be able to accuse me of disbelief."

"No . . . well . . . it was one of those messy cases," she broke out. "Cruelty. Not violence, you know, I've forgotten the phrase, but it meant . . . it meant—"

"She said his conduct towards her was injuring her health," he suggested; but he was thinking that the accusation might cover a multitude of sins.

"Something like that," said Barbara.

"Did Mr. Canning defend the suit?"

"Oh, yes, he did. He was afraid, you see . . . he didn't want to lose Clare. That's what made it so beastly. But he ought to have known they'd believe what Laura said."

"You didn't feel, yourself, that perhaps she was justified?"

"No, I didn't." She spoke shortly. "But I admit, I'm prejudiced."

"Why?"

"Well, because . . . that's opinion again, Mr. Maitland, and if it isn't obvious I can't tell you."

"Because you feel that sometimes Laura misunderstood, or at any rate misrepresented, the things you did?"

"Well ... perhaps." Her tone was grudging.

"Where is Clare now?"

"With her father. He married again, eighteen months ago. She'll be all right with Emmie."

"And Laura, too, was thinking of remarrying?"

"It doesn't sound much as though she committed suicide, does it?" she said, putting his thought into words. "And really, Mr. Maitland, I do think you should forget about that possibility. She'd never have gone down to the kitchen to wash the glass after she took her medicine. And if she had done, she wouldn't have hung up her dressing gown again; she'd have left it for someone else to put away. Laura was like that; things had always been easy for her."

Always? thought Antony. The divorce, at least, must have been distressing to any woman with sensitivity. But on the other hand .... "If you're so sure about that," he said, deliberately, "what do you think happened?"

She was looking dreamily at a point beyond his shoulder as she answered. "I don't know. I don't know at all. Perhaps it was an accident." The green eyes came into focus again and met his with a look that was disturbing, even faintly tinged with mockery. "But we don't have to prove anything, do we? *They've* got to prove I'm guilty."

3

AS IT WAS SATURDAY, the Maitlands should have been lunching with Sir Nicholas; but Antony was feeling confused, and even a little ruffled after his talk with Barbara Wentworth, and rather balked at further discussion until he had had time to think things out. Instead, he phoned Jenny to tell her what he was doing, and he had an unappetizing meal in a tearoom because he was too preoccupied to do anything but turn into the first place he saw. The only thing to be thankful for was that he had had presence of mind to refuse Mr. Bellerby's invitation. The solicitor had welcomed him with enthusiasm that morning but now seemed to be doubting his own wisdom. "I've never known you so unkind," he said; and though he refrained from further recrimination, his eyes were reproachful.

So Antony lunched alone and was annoyed to find when he had finished that he had done no constructive thinking at all. He went away to find a phone, and dialed Derek Stringer's number; and tried to decide, when he heard his friend reply, whether there was anything—anything at all—in Uncle Nick's notion. He couldn't help feeling Derek's greeting was unenthusiastic; or it might be imagination; or it might be true, and still nothing to the point.

"Sir Nicholas told me," said Stringer, "that he's asked you to take a hand with the Wentworth brief." Perhaps he was piqued, Antony thought, but they'd worked together so often it didn't seem likely . . . .

"Do you mind?" he asked.

"Of course not. Why should I?" But suddenly he was angry, and the anger sounded in his voice. "I just don't think this is the occasion for one of your damned crusades."

"I'm sorry you feel that," said Antony. "But if we can uncover some additional evidence—"

"Don't you think it's a little late for that?"

"It may be. Are you saying she's guilty, Derek?"

"You know our line," said Stringer. He may not have intended the words to sound quite so much like a sneer. "Of course she's innocent."

"Well, be that as it may," said Antony, "I've promised Uncle Nick, and I've got to start somewhere." His intentions were pacific, but his words seemed only to have an inflammatory effect.

"I just don't agree that it's going to be helpful."

"No. You've made that clear enough." Not a doubt of it, something was up with Derek. And he only hoped Uncle Nick was wrong in his diagnosis; the situation was complicated enough as it was. "I've seen Miss Wentworth, and I've been through Uncle Nick's notes," he added. "And now I need your help."

"I . . . look here, Antony, I'm sorry," said Stringer, in a rush. "It's just that I've thought and thought about this business, and I don't see my way at all."

"It isn't easy," Antony agreed.

"Easy!" said Stringer. He was silent for a moment and then added, less explosively, "You say you've been to the prison. What did you think of her?"

"I don't really know," said Antony, carefully. "Not yet. She's very beautiful," he added.

"I suppose she is."

"And helpful . . . up to a point. But what I want now is some addresses."

"Where are you going to start?" The interest in Derek's tone might be grudging, but it was the first time he had shown any at all.

"I want to find out what Laura Canning was really like," Antony told him and was startled by the sudden crackle of laughter in his ear.

"According to the prosecution, an angel straight from heaven."

"I wonder if that view was shared by all her acquaintances," said Antony, thoughtfully.

"I daresay not. But it won't help the defense to blacken the victim's character," Stringer pointed out.

"That wasn't what I had in mind . . . not exactly," said Antony, mildly enough. "I want to know what she was really like," he repeated. "And her sister, too, for that matter. I gather the other people in the house are being called—"

"Mrs. Mills and her niece. Yes, they are. And that chap Prior . . . who sounds a perfect swine," said Stringer, viciously.

"His evidence should be interesting, anyway. But in the meantime . . . some friends of Laura's now, whom the prosecution have no use for."

"There's a Miss Stuart, who lives in Putney. And a couple called Newton, who were her neighbors in Roehampton. I can find their addresses—though I can't think why you didn't get them from Bellerby—but what they have to say isn't evidence," he added, gloomily.

"That doesn't matter. Did they know the Cannings—both of them—before the divorce?"

"I think so. They were living in the same place; Laura just kept the flat on after they separated."

"I see. And what about Barbara? She worked at a shop called Raymonde's."

"Her employer's an odd sort of type." Derek was speaking more freely now, but still there was an undertone of reluctance. "Invariably referred to as *madame* . . . French as they come . . . married name, O'Toole, seems rather incongruous."

"I can see it might, I'll start with her, Derek."

"I said she was odd. She may have a certain amusement value," said Stringer, acidly, "but there isn't anything we could call her for, except evidence as to character. And that isn't really in question."

"All the same, *I* want to know. And I call that downright cynical," said Antony. "What about the other two girls who work there?"

"Jill and Dorothy. I can't remember their other names. They shared a flat with Barbara, so I suppose they know her pretty well. But, even so . . . the trial started yesterday; if you're going to find anything to help, it's got to be done quickly."

"Well . . . where would you suggest I start?" But that wasn't really fair. After all, Derek had made his position clear enough. "Just find me those addresses," he promised, "and I won't bother you any more."

Raymonde's, in Knightsbridge, shows an elegant face to the world. Antony had phoned ahead, and madame was expecting him; she let him in by the main door and led him through the hushed elegance of the showroom, through the bleaker, more congested area at the back, to her own quarters on the first floor.

She talked as they went ... never, never, never did those girls *ranger ses choses comme il faut*. They should go tomorrow, ah, no, that was the day of rest ... they should go at the end of the week, but what then? She could find no one to help her whose faults would not be a thousand times worse. Here, now, was her *petit salon* ... this floor she kept for herself. Upstairs was for *les couseuses*, but not at weekends ... no overtime ... that was understood. To pay extra for such simple work ... one would be ruined.

To the masculine eye, all seemed in order. Madame herself was short and shapeless, even though a certain rigidity in her bearing suggested that she was pretty well armor-plated under her well-cut black wool dress. She had boot-black hair, which she wore piled on top of her head in an erection rather like a cottage loaf; a plain, heavy face; snapping black eyes; and all the energy and vivacity of her race.

There was an appraising look for her visitor as she seated herself in a big, old-fashioned armchair, managing to do so regally in spite of her skirt, which was fashionably skimpy. "Put yourself at ease, *m'sieur*. You have come to tell me good news of this Barbara, I think."

"I'm afraid not, *madame*."

The dark eyes were reproachful. *"Eh bien, m'sieur?"*

"I have come to ask your help."

"But I know nothing—nothing!—of this *affaire*."

"That, *madame*, I understand very well. But you know Miss Barbara Wentworth."

"And I have told them ... the lawyers ... all that I know of her."

"It is a fault in me, no doubt. I like to hear for myself." To his surprise she nodded vigorously.

"But I agree ... if there was anything—"

"Tell me about Barbara Wentworth, *madame*."

"What is there to tell? She is beautiful ... if you have seen her there is no need to tell you this. She is ... that so disagreeable word you have in English ... *capable*—"

"Efficient, *madame*?"

"She is efficient. And that, I will tell you, is a good thing because I ... I am not efficient at all. When she came to me, six, seven years ago, she is just a little girl who has learned how to walk, how to wear her clothes. Business ... *pouf!*" said madame, gesturing vigorously. "But she has a head, that one. She learns quickly . . . where to buy, what to buy. If I say, this gown is not the fashion, or that one is ugly, she tell me, 'This will suit Mme Black *à merveille*; and Mme White is without taste, won't you see if she will buy that one?' And — *mon dieu!* — she is right. And then, after a while, she finds out that I do not like *les comptes.*"

"So she took over the bookkeeping too?"

"That is what I am telling you. And soon there is money in the bank . . . even though I pay those girls two, three times more than they are worth," she added, with a certain amount of venom in her tone.

"Well, that is Miss Wentworth as an employee. As a person, now — ?"

"What can I tell you?" madame demanded. "She has a cool head and a warm heart. And it is madness, *m'sieur*, madness to say that she would kill her sister. In a passion . . . who knows? But with poison, with the child in the house . . . no, and no, and no!"

"She is capable of passion, then?"

"But, yes! I say she is cool; that is, as to business. I do not say she is an iceberg," madame pointed out scornfully.

"Her friends?"

"Now will you believe me when I say that I think first of those silly girls? They shared an apartment, and there are conveniences, I suppose, but I do not understand such a *ménage.*"

"The other two are still living in the same place?"

"They are silly girls, *m'sieur*, and can tell you nothing. But . . . yes, they are still in the same place."

"There was someone she mentioned, someone who helped her. A model, I think, but older than herself."

"I do not know of any other women friends than Jill and Dorothy. As for her escorts . . . they go and come, *m'sieur.*"

"Did she ever speak of Stanley Prior?"

For the first time she hesitated over her answer. "She did not speak of her friends . . . ever," she said at last. "But him I have met here, when he has called for her."

"What did you think of him?"

"A type I understand very well." Her tone was dry. "Charming, a man of the world."

"Wealthy?"

"He behaves like a wealthy man, *m'sieur*. Impossible *à dire.*"

"Did you get the impression they knew each other well?" He wasn't surprised when she burst out laughing.

"That is tact, is it not? What you really want to know—"

"As you understand so well, *madame* ... won't you tell me?"

"I think he was *épris*. But as for Barbara ... he lit no lamps for her, *m'sieur*. So I do not think they were lovers, but I do not know."

"You have heard it said he was going to marry Mrs. Canning?"

"I have heard it." She set her lips, but after a moment burst out with all her normal loquacity. "She had the money, that one ... that Laura. And he understood very well, I think, that one should have a care for the future."

"Did you know her?"

"Oh, yes ... oh, yes. I knew her very well."

Now what was it in her tone that rang untrue? A bitterness, perhaps ... an animosity that took her knowledge of the dead woman out of the range of the casual. "How was that?" he asked cautiously.

"She came to the *salon*. Was that strange, when her sister worked here for so many years?"

"She came as a customer?"

"As a client ... yes. At other times, too. She was worried about Barbara, she said; but I think," said madame shrewdly, "she would have been satisfied to find there was something wrong."

"You didn't like her?"

"As to that ... she was inquisitive, a little," she replied, again with that unfamiliar note of caution. There was something else, if only he could hit on the right questions; but why should she answer him, after all, or tell him anything she didn't want to? But, he thought, for her it was easier to speak than to be silent.

"Had Mrs. Canning's visits been going on for long?"

"Almost as long as Barbara had been here." She saw a possible detour, and rushed down it with enthusiasm. "You will understand, *m'sieur*, it was a pleasure to dress her. She was a fair, pretty woman, always beautifully neat. She had a good figure, and she knew—as so many women do not—exactly what would suit her."

"Was Miss Wentworth pleased to see her sister?"

"I cannot tell. She was not demonstrative, that one."

"If Mrs. Canning was inquisitive ... you mean, about her sister's affairs?"

"Yes." It was the note of relief in her tone that prompted the additional question.

"In other matters, too?"

"Enfin, elle ne devait pas fourrer son nez dans mes affairs."

Antony frowned. "You mean, she asked you questions about the business?" he hazarded. And again the look of relief was unmistakable.

"She said she wished to invest," madame told him.

"In the shop?" For some reason, the statement had surprised him; and the question shot out more forcefully than he had intended. She had a cold look for his violence.

"But why not?" she asked.

"No reason at all. I'm sure from her point of view ... but would you have liked a partner, *madame?*"

"As to that, she did not intend to concern herself with the business, you understand." She shrugged as she spoke. "And one must, after all, be sensible."

"It was arranged then, this partnership?"

"But, no. Nothing of the kind. Nothing final. When the suggestion has been made I have told Barbara, and always she has said I must not do it."

"You listened to her objections?"

"I did not want to lose her," said madame simply. "And she would have left me, *m'sieur,* without any doubt at all."

"Because she disliked her sister?"

"That was not my affair, *m'sieur.* She said only, 'I will not be tied,' and she looked ... very angry."

"You did not see Mrs. Canning while she was ill ... the fortnight before she died?"

"Our relationship was not a social one, *m'sieur. Elle m'aurait rapelée quand elle y était prête.*"

Now, what exactly did she mean by that? He found himself stumbling over his next question and hoped she would think it was because he was occupied with the difficulties of translation. "And—and the day she died had Miss Wentworth been to work as usual?"

"Yes. Everything was as usual, except that she would hurry away in the evening. It was farther to go, you see, to Laura's apartment, and *la bonne* in a hurry, always, to get away."

"Nothing strange?" he persisted. "Nothing that she told you—"

"I have said, she was not one for confidences."

"—nothing that you could, yourself, observe in her manner?"

"Mais non, m'sieur, Je vous ai dit déjà bien des fois qu'il n'y avait rien."

Now, why should that excite her? He was quite sure she had again dropped into her own language deliberately, and his expression became wooden. "There was ... nothing," he said, as though essaying a tentative translation. He sighed and got to his feet. "I didn't expect anything, really," he told her.

"If I could have helped, *m'sieur,* I should have been very happy." She got up in her turn and began to move across the room.

"And this ... curiosity of Mrs. Canning's." He was following her slowly, and she turned with her hand on the door to answer him.

"J'étais au bout de mes forces. Mais, quoi faire? Elle l'emportait sur moi complètement." The vehemence died. She shrugged and said calmly, *"Mille pardons, m'sieur.* I forget—"

"When you speak so quickly—" said Antony, stopping there to avoid a direct lie.

"I say only, some women are like that. When they have not enough to do." She pulled the door open as she spoke. "And that, too, I have told you already," she added reproachfully. And preceded him in silence down the stairs.

4

OUTSIDE THE DAY, which had started disagreeably, showed signs of ending—even more unpleasantly for all concerned—in a light fog. Antony, realizing for the first time as he reached the street that Madame Raymonde's apartment had been heated to an almost transatlantic intensity, turned up his collar and set out on foot, by the route he had previously mapped out for himself, for his next port of call. Inevitably, because he didn't want them, he was confronted by a succession of half-empty buses, any of which would have taken him fairly near home. He thought a little wistfully of tea and crumpets and a good fire; Uncle Nick, confound him, would be enjoying all three, and if he boarded the next of those tantalizing buses ... he put the temptation behind him, and went on.

He wondered when he reached the place if Barbara Wentworth (or Jill, or Dorothy) had carefully chosen her residence to be near, but not too near, the shop. Enough exercise to help maintain the trimness of figure a model required; not so far as to prove daunting after a hard day's work. In the porch, the top bell said "Wentworth," thus still preserving the other two girls' anonymity. He pressed it hopefully, and after a moment there was a loud clicking sound, and when he tried the inner door it was open.

It seemed a good bet that the flat was at the top of the house, so after hesitating briefly in the hall he began to mount the stairs. On each landing closed doors confronted him; the house was silent and cold and grudgingly lit, and smelled of furniture polish and cabbage. From which he deduced (though the logic is not quite apparent) that the landlady lived in the basement.

But when he reached the top flight there was a change of atmosphere. At the top was a small, square landing, so brightly lighted that the illumination spilled generously down the dark staircase. A fair-haired girl in a blue dressing gown was leaning dangerously over the rails; she gave a startled squeak when she saw him and said in consternation, "Oh, no! I thought you were Margie."

He couldn't see her face, but the light shining behind her gave distinctly the effect of a halo. "'And the stars in her hairs were seven,'" he murmured—the impulse being quite irresistible—and stopped, looking up at her.

"What on earth—? Who do you want?" she demanded.

"I'm looking for—" oh, Lord, he'd forgotten their names "—for Miss Wentworth's apartment. I want to talk to her friends."

She moved a little nearer the head of the stairs, as though to bar his progress if he decided to come any farther. "Why?" she asked. "This is the right place, but ... why?"

"I should have phoned," said Antony, "but I didn't quite know what time I'd get here." (He hoped he wasn't going to have to conduct the whole interview as a sort of balcony scene.) "My name's Maitland, and I'm associated with Miss Wentworth's counsel ... my uncle's defending her. May I come up?"

"Yes ... yes, of course." But she moved rather slowly from her defensive position and seemed to be regarding him warily as he mounted the remaining steps. When he reached the landing he stopped to look at her, and as she turned he saw her face clearly for the first time. Not the Blessed Damozel after all ... a dreary female he'd always thought her, anyway. This girl had a round face, and a snub nose, and a mouth too full for beauty. One of the cherubim, perhaps? But when she smiled at him, as she did after a moment's grave scrutiny, her whole face lighted up with an amusement that didn't seem altogether angelic. "I don't understand at all," she said, "but you'd better come in." And she moved ahead of him toward the open door of a room at the front of the house.

It was a long room with dormer windows, cheerfully furnished in a chintzy sort of way. It was warm, and not very tidy, and—like the landing—brightly lit. The fair girl went across to a door at the far end, opened it, and uttered a piercing shriek that might have been wordless for all the sense it conveyed to Antony. She came back then, and sat down near the electric fire, and waved him to the chair opposite her. "I'm Jill Chesson," she said. "Dorothy will be out in a moment. I was just warning her," she explained. "And now, will you tell me—"

It wasn't very easy to explain why he had come, since he wasn't altogether convinced himself that his researches would have any good effect. He didn't want to raise false hopes, and he didn't want to cast her into a gloom; and for all her surface gaiety he could sense her anxiety. When he had finished she sat looking at him in silence for a moment and then said abruptly, "I could make some tea, but it's such a beastly day I expect you'd rather have something stronger. If you can drink gin——"

Antony signified his ability to drink gin, and let his eyes wander round the room as she went across to an old-fashioned buffet. There was a conflict of personalities here, and he wondered which of the three girls was responsible for the basic furnishings, which of them had introduced the paintings—reproductions, he supposed; there was a landscape over the fireplace, and the remainder were flower studies, but they all had a clarity of color and line which he found attractive—and which of them owned the Doulton figures dancing their way across the mantelpiece. The bookshelves might have provided further mystification, if he had had time to study them, but Jill was a quick worker and came back to the hearth with two glasses before he had time to extend his research.

"Dorothy will be here in a minute," she repeated. "I'm sorry we're in such a mess——" (she picked up a towel from the floor, and a comb from the arm of the sofa, and tucked both out of sight under a cushion) "—but she has a date tonight, so I was doing her hair."

"I'm afraid——" said Antony, but she cut the apology short.

"We've hours yet. It's just that I've promised to be out of here by seven . . . and to leave their supper ready," she added with a grin. "I've made them a casserole—can you smell it?" Antony, who had been conscious for some time that the odor of cabbage had been replaced by something extremely savory, nodded and leaned back in his chair. It seemed they must wait for Dorothy before the real business of the meeting began.

Dorothy was a brunette. Her hair was thick and straight and carefully arranged, though to Antony's irreverent mind it suggested a triumph of the topiarist's art rather than that of the hairdresser. Her face was an almost perfect oval, and her features were good, if a little heavy. She was dressed with rather more propriety than Jill, having on a long, navy blue housecoat; and she gave the other girl's faded wrapper a reproving look as she sank down onto the sofa.

"You ought to go and change," she said.

"Later," said Jill, with only a touch of impatience. "This is Mr. Maitland, Dorothy. I thought he was mad at first, but now he doesn't seem to be." The dark girl's eyes turned consideringly in Antony's direction. "He's a lawyer, and he's on Barbara's side, and he wants to talk to us."

Dorothy smiled at the visitor. "We shall be glad to do anything we can," she told him graciously, and relaxed against the cushions. He was to recall later that she accepted his inquiries more easily than anybody else; but he did not think it was her nature to take a questioning view of life.

"Now!" said Jill.

He started off slowly, with some routine questions. It was Jill who did the talking, with Dorothy nodding her acquiescence when appealed to from time to time; and after a while she came to need less prompting, to speak more freely. "You all three work at Raymonde's?" he asked them.

"Yes. Of course, Dorothy and I are just models . . . Barbara knew everything about the business. Have you seen madame?"

"I have," he said, and smiled at her.

"What did she tell you?"

"That Barbara was efficient."

She paused to consider this statement. "Yes . . . well . . . I think she liked her. But she's an awfully keen businesswoman, Mr. Maitland. I'm always afraid she might decide to . . . to—"

"To throw Barbara to the wolves?"

"Something like that. Not that I suppose she could do her much harm now," she added sadly.

"Have you been with her long? Do you know her background?"

"Barbara was there first, and then Dorothy, and I've been there nearly four years now. As for her background, I don't wonder you're curious. She married Mr. O'Toole ages ago—"

"How long?"

"Well, before the war, anyway. And he died in about 1950, and she used what he left her to start the shop . . . at least, that's what she always says. But whether she came to England to marry him or was here already, I just don't know."

"If you've stayed there so long, you must like working for her," Antony suggested.

"It's a job," said Jill. She glanced uncertainly at her friend, but Dorothy had closed her eyes. "I'd think twice about moving," she went on, "because good jobs are hard to find. But I'd never have left while Barbara was there."

"That goes for me, too," said Dorothy. When he turned to look at her, she was eyeing him steadily. "There's nothing really wrong with madame," she added, "except that she looks out for herself; we all have to do that."

"Did you know that Mrs. Canning was thinking of putting capital into the business?"

"Yes, Barbara told us. She was furious," Jill told him. And then broke off and gave him a hostile look, as though he were somehow to blame for the indiscretion. "It was just," she added, "that she liked to be independent."

Antony said quietly, "You said yourself, Miss Chesson, that I was 'on Barbara's side.' "

"Yes, but . . . is that the same as believing her?" she asked. He smiled at her challenging tone.

"It needn't be," he admitted.

"Have you seen her, Mr. Maitland?"

"This morning . . . for the first time."

Perhaps he stressed the last words slightly, for she flashed back at him. "I'm not prejudiced. I'm not! Barbara wouldn't—"

"I didn't say I disbelieved her." But he knew as he spoke that he'd be happier if he thought she'd told him all the truth. Jill was still bristling . . . not a cherub, he thought again, with amusement. He turned to look at Dorothy, and found her dark eyes fixed on him anxiously.

"She's right, you know," she said in her slow way. "It may sound silly, but . . . Barbara wouldn't."

"That's what we're hoping to prove," he told her. His tone masked his irritation well enough. "But an opinion based on character . . . we can't produce that in court."

"I know," Jill agreed. "That's what the solicitor . . . what Mr. Bellerby told us."

But Dorothy burst out, with almost as much vigor as her friend had previously used, "It's dreadful! They'll put her in prison for years and years; that's all her life gone, wasted. How could she start again, ever? I don't know how she could bear it."

Antony made an abrupt movement, throwing out his hand as though to stop what she was saying. He knew in that instant, as he should have known before, that he wouldn't rest now until he knew the truth of Laura Canning's death; and that he would find it quite intolerable to believe in Barbara's innocence unless it was possible to prove it. The atmosphere of the prison was still vividly in his mind. To face that for years, with freedom no more than a bitter memory . . . .

The two girls were staring, and he realized that the silence had lengthened between them. "All right then," he said, roughly. "What do you think happened?"

"It must have been an accident," said Jill; but she spoke in a small voice, almost guiltily, and her tone carried no conviction at all.

"That doesn't seem very likely," Dorothy objected. "Somebody did it . . . not Barbara . . . and if I knew who, I'd tell you." She leaned back again and closed her eyes, but Antony was beginning to suspect that pose.

"You knew Mrs. Canning," he said. "What was she like?"

"She was very pretty," Jill told him, after a glance at her friend had assured her that the floor was hers again. "And she dressed beautifully; her clothes must have cost a fortune."

"He means, what was she *like?*" Dorothy sounded sleepy.

"I'm telling him. She was . . . well, she meant well," said Jill. "She was always very nice to us—"

"Condescending," said Dorothy.

"—and if she did seem to interfere a little, it was only because she worried about Barbara."

"How did she interfere?"

"Well . . . she didn't really, I suppose, because Barbara didn't take any notice. But she tried to get her to live in a club, or in a 'respectable guesthouse,' and she was always asking her about her friends. As if she was a child."

"You haven't told him about the time she came here."

Jill hesitated. "She did rather poke around," she admitted. "And she said we'd be better with modern furniture, and the paintings were commonplace, and there was room on the landing for a big cupboard that would take lots of our rubbish."

"And we didn't use the right kind of cosmetics, and it was extravagant to buy frozen vegetables." Dorothy's indignation had apparently woken her up again. "Jill's a marvelous cook," she added. "but when you're working, you have to do things the easy way. Of course, what Laura *really* wanted," the dark girl went on, reflectively, "was to find out if we were living in sin."

Antony resisted the temptation to ask, "And were you?" which perhaps was just as well, for Jill gasped, "Dorothy!" and sounded really shocked.

Dorothy smiled benignly at the visitor, and said in her deep voice, "She didn't know Mother Superior here." The slightest of gestures indicated her friend. "She has principles, you know." Her tone might be gently teasing, but there was no doubt that it also held affection.

"Well!" said Jill. She was sitting bolt upright on the edge of her chair, her face was flushed, and she had pushed her hair back from her forehead until it stood up in a fantastic coxcomb. She looked, for the moment, about sixteen, and anything but prudish. "Anyone would think," she said, and her voice trembled with indignation, "that you and Barbara—"

"Madame told me," Antony intervened hastily, "that Miss Wentworth wasn't really interested in this fellow—what's-his-name?—Stanley Prior."

Dorothy gave him an approving look. "She was quite right," she told him. "I'm glad you understand."

"Well, I don't," said Jill. "He's a fascinating person, and I don't know how she could resist him." The effort to sound like a woman of the world, in view of the unglamorous picture she presented, was decidedly comical. But a moment later she had forgotten both her dignity and her grievance. "Was it true he was going to marry Laura?" she asked.

"What makes you think so?"

"I . . . it was only a guess. And I asked Mr. Bellerby, but I don't think he likes answering questions."

"Neither does Mr. Maitland," said Dorothy, watching him.

"I'm being as nosy as Laura," said Jill, contritely. "But I'll tell you this, anyway: if he'd asked her, she'd have had him."

"Had he known Barbara a long time?"

"Oh, ages. Three years, anyway. He's very amusing, you know. They used to go out together a lot."

"She liked him," said Dorothy, unexpectedly, "because he appreciated her brain, not just her looks. But that doesn't mean she was in love with him."

"Would you say he's conceited?"

"Oh, no!" said Jill.

At exactly the same moment as her friend replied, "Yes. But I think," Dorothy added, obviously trying to be fair, "that most men would be, with his looks and . . . and address."

"What is his occupation?"

Again both girls started to speak together, and then stopped and exchanged a doubtful look. "We don't really know," said Jill. "Now I think of it, he seems to have a good deal of spare time."

"I thought he had something to do with the rag trade," said Dorothy. "Clothes," she added, in case the visitor had misunderstood her. "But I don't know his firm, so perhaps I'm wrong about that."

Antony was beginning to have a hearty dislike for the absent Mr. Prior. He said, reflectively, "Never mind. What about Douglas Canning? Do you know him, too?" He looked from one to the other of them, but they both shook their heads.

"All we know," said Jill after a moment, "is what Barbara told us from time to time. I mean, we knew about the divorce, and I think Barbara used to see him sometimes, even after that."

"He used to talk to her about his little girl, about Clare," Dorothy put in.

"It was Mrs. Canning who brought suit ... who was the injured party?"

"I suppose so. At any rate, Clare stayed with her mother."

"Barbara used to take her out sometimes at the weekends." Jill seemed to have recovered her spirits. "I've been with them to the zoo, and to the toy departments at Christmas; we used to have great fun. She's a nice child, but a little nervous."

"So would you be," said Dorothy, who seemed refreshingly free from any of the usual inhibitions about speaking of the dead, "if you'd had to live with Laura Canning."

"After all, she was her mother." The protest might be a routine one, but Jill's eyes were troubled. "I've been wondering about Clare ... it's such an upset, and then her father married again, you know."

"If I hear anything of her, I'll tell you," Antony promised. He twisted in his chair to pick up the glass that, so far, had been standing neglected at his elbow. "I ought to be going, I've disturbed your plans enough as it is."

"If only we could have helped," said Jill, mournfully. "And there's no hurry, really. The meal's all ready," she told Dorothy. The thought seemed to cheer her. "And if you let Mark think you cooked it, you'll be the most deceitful thing alive."

They watched him in silence while he finished his drink, but he thought something had disturbed the friendly atmosphere of the

long, untidy room. When he got up at last Jill started toward the
door that led to the landing, but Dorothy said, quite briskly, "It's
high time you changed," and she stopped, docilely enough, gave
Antony her hand and murmured something and whisked herself
out of the other door. The dark girl went, without haste, to pick up
the visitor's overcoat, which her friend had thrown down on one
of the dining chairs, and held it for him in silence.

Then, apparently reaching a decision, she looked up at him and
said in her quiet way, "She trusts everyone."

Antony smiled at her. "She even trusted me, once she decided I
wasn't mad," he agreed. But she wasn't immediately to be
diverted.

"I hope she was right about that," she said. "I hope we were
both right. But I was wondering, Mr. Maitland . . . your coming
here now, after the trial has started—"

"What about it?"

"Has something new come up, or is it a—a sort of forlorn
hope?" she asked him.

"Nothing new, I'm afraid." He wished he could reassure her, but
even to say, "Don't worry" would be to give too much encouragement. "She has very able counsel, you know. Everything possible
is being done."

"Yes, I'm sure . . . I've heard of Sir Nicholas Harding," she said.
"But no one can make bricks without straw." She spoke so
gravely that it wasn't till later he realized the triteness of the
phrase.

"Well, that's what I'm doing . . . trying to find the straw," he
told her. And this time she returned his smile. But as he let himself
out into the cold street again the memory of her troubled look
disturbed him, until he thought of Jill, with her childlike face and
her flair for cookery. Then he grinned to himself and decided to
take a taxi home. Madame might not understand "such a
ménage," but he thought Jenny would find an account of it
amusing.

Up till then it hadn't really mattered to him; but now, for the
first time, he had begun consciously to hope that Barbara
Wentworth was innocent.

5

JENNY LOOKED AT HER HUSBAND thoughtfully when he had finished his description of the day's activities. "I rather thought you'd find it was hopeless," she said. "But you've decided to go on, haven't you?"

"I felt it was hopeless from the beginning. I still do. After all, I don't even know whether she's innocent or guilty." Antony got up restlessly and began to walk about the room. "Uncle Nick baited a trap for me," he said, after a moment. "And I walked into it with my eyes open, so I shouldn't complain. But there's no going back now."

"Why not?" She thought she knew the answer to that, but if he was in a mood to talk . . . .

"Because . . . if she is innocent . . . I can't just leave it there, without knowing." He paused by the window, and lifted the curtain and peered out; the fog had thickened now, and the street lamp on the corner was only a blur in the surrounding gloom. "She wouldn't ask for help," he said, dropping the curtain and coming back toward the fire. "And Derek told me it wasn't the occasion for one of my damned crusades."

"That wasn't very nice of him," said Jenny, severely.

His expression lightened. "He may be right at that."

"At least you're doing something. And all he does is dither; at least that's what Uncle Nick says."

"Something's wrong," Antony admitted. "But I hope to goodness Uncle Nick isn't right about his being in love with the girl; I've no real desire to mix myself up in his affairs."

"It isn't his affair, anyway," Jenny pointed out.

"No, but . . . the principle's the same."

"Well, I've got a nasty feeling . . . I think he's afraid to believe she's innocent, because then if she was convicted he'd find it quite unbearable."

There was something uncanny in this echo of his own thought. "But he wouldn't need to have fallen for her to feel like that."

"*You* wouldn't, Antony; I think Derek would. He hasn't got such a—a strong sense of abstract justice as you have."

He looked at her blankly for a moment, and then he laughed, as perhaps she had intended. But when he thought about it later, he was still just as uneasy on his friend's behalf.

SIR NICHOLAS had summoned his junior to a conference the next morning, and had commanded also his nephew's attendance. Antony was, consequently, in rather a querulous frame of mind when he went down to the study, soon after eleven. "If Derek goes mad and bites me," he said, "don't say I didn't warn you."

But Derek Stringer, arriving a few minutes later with a bulging briefcase, seemed to have forgotten the rancor of their talk the day before. He was a tall man, too thin for his height, and looking older than he really was because of a receding hair line. He was medium dark, and generally very pale; but for all that he was capable of tireless bursts of energy which had been known to reduce his colleagues to a state of exhaustion. Unexpectedly, he had rather mild, brown eyes, which gave him a deceptively tranquil look. Antony, looking at him this morning with unusual perception, thought that from his serious demeanor a stranger would never realize one half of the zest and sheer enjoyment he brought to life. He thought, too, that Derek had followed him unquestioningly, and almost without protest, through a good many unlikely situations and he wondered uneasily whether, in this case, all that would be changed. But perhaps the fact that Stringer had backed him in the past was odder in itself than his attitude the day before. He was exceptionally quick-witted, and certainly not without opinions of his own.

However that might be, he was behaving now with determined propriety. Perhaps, after all, the whole thing had been imagination; anyone might be bad-tempered one day of the year. But it wasn't really like Uncle Nick to start a hare like that.

"I went through everything after I talked to you yesterday," said Stringer, taking the chair his leader indicated and setting the briefcase down with a thump beside him. "I think the people I mentioned are the best ones for you to start with."

Sir Nicholas was sitting behind the desk and had put on his

glasses, the better, apparently, to admire the family of ducks he was drawing on his blotting pad. He looked up now at his nephew. "You didn't tell me you had decided on a starting point," he remarked.

"I didn't have time," Antony pointed out. "But what do you think I was doing yesterday?" As usual on these occasions, he preferred to remain mobile unless adjured pretty strongly to sit down. He was standing at the corner of the desk and had pulled a bundle of old envelopes out of his pocket, from which he selected at last, with an air of relief, one which seemed to have nothing in particular to recommend it except some illegible pencil scrawls across the back.

"If you really want to play guessing games," said Sir Nicholas, disagreeably, "I should say you were frivoling. Don't tell me," he added, as Antony opened his mouth to refute the charge, "that you didn't go to see those girls—what do they call themselves?—the two from the shop."

"It was the logical starting place." Antony's eyes met Derek's, and they exchanged a look of amused understanding. He glanced down at his envelope again. "Roehampton?" he said. "Shall we go and see these people this afternoon, Derek? Then you can show me Laura's flat, as well."

"If you like." He didn't sound enthusiastic.

Sir Nicholas said, with sharp irritation. "I can see nothing against it, if Stringer wishes to accompany you. But will it help?"

"He knows the background, sir. And I have to start somewhere," he added, trying to forestall the further query he knew his uncle had in mind. He thought, too, "I'd have taken him with me yesterday if he hadn't bitten my head off." But he did not say it.

"Very well. Now, before we get down to tomorrow's tactics, did anything strike you when you talked to those girls yesterday?"

"Nothing much. They're rather nice girls really, Uncle Nick."

Sir Nicholas removed his spectacles, the better to glare at his nephew. "They may be a couple of plaster saints, though I doubt it," he said unpleasantly. "The point is, did they tell you anything?"

"Only that they don't altogether agree about people. Dorothy says Jill's too trusting."

"About whom do they disagree?"

"Laura Canning, for one. Jill thinks she meant well; the other girl isn't so sure." He paused for so long that Sir Nicholas's expression became ominous. "They didn't agree about Stanley Prior either," he said at last.

"About his character?"

"About whether he is conceited." Sir Nicholas raised his eyes to heaven and appeared to be praying. Antony said, suddenly exasperated, "It happens to be a material point, sir. I did other things yesterday besides ... frivol."

"Such as?"

"You know perfectly well I went to see Barbara Wentworth."

"Come to the point, Antony; if there is a point."

"This chap Prior is being called by the prosecution—"

"The fact had not escaped me."

"—and one of the things they'll ask him is whether there was any friction between the two sisters because of him. They'll also ask him about his date with Barbara the night Laura died." Sir Nicholas grasped his pencil again and started a fresh assault on his blotting pad. "Well, that was when he told her he was going to propose to Laura ... he was breaking it to her because he thought the news would upset her ... don't you think the jury will be interested in that?"

Stringer growled something under his breath. Sir Nicholas said gently, his eyes on his sketch, "I admit I did not expect your efforts would be confined to—er—sabotaging the defense."

"It's better to know, sir. Isn't it?"

"Decidedly. What other helpful points did Miss Wentworth mention that she had previously forgotten?"

Antony eyed him uneasily. "I think you should realize it's a thing she's sensitive about," he said.

"As my efforts will be directed to minimizing the effects of the prosecution's case, you needn't really be afraid I shall do anything to offend the lady's sensibilities," said Sir Nicholas, coldly.

"No, sir. Nothing else was even potentially helpful, except that Douglas Canning once told her that Laura had threatened to take her own life. The prosecution aren't calling him. Are you?"

Sir Nicholas looked across at his junior and then applied himself again to his sketch. Stringer said, as though unwillingly, "We considered it, of course. But we thought ... on the whole ... it wouldn't be very helpful."

The newest duck was admiring its reflection in a puddle of

water. "The divorce was not an amicable one," Sir Nicholas observed, "and I think his testimony would be suspect. It should prove more effective to rely on the medical evidence." He leaned back a little to consider his handiwork.

"Have you any?" asked Antony bluntly.

This time it was Derek who replied, without prompting. "Any doctor who ever had anything to do with Laura, alive or dead, is already being called by the prosecution," he said, bitterly.

"We must do what we can in cross-examination," Sir Nicholas added. "I am looking forward in particular to questioning the—er—deceased members of the profession."

"And the child? I should have thought Lamb would want her evidence."

"No need for that." The pencil went down on the blotter; just for the moment Sir Nicholas seemed to be giving the discussion his full attention. "In suggesting opportunity he has only to describe Miss Wentworth's return to the flat ... the visiting neighbor already gone ... the sleeping child—"

"But—"

"It's up to us to prove the contrary. Clare Canning says—you must have her statement there, Stringer—that she went to sleep and stayed asleep. But even if her evidence would be helpful, I doubt if our client would let us call her."

"I see. Well, I hope the father will be more accommodating. What were the grounds for the divorce, Derek?"

"Cruelty. One of those vague, unsatisfactory cases, with the wife playing the injured innocent—"

"Which may have been true, for all we know."

"—and the husband protesting far too much for his own good, or dignity."

"Ah, well. *Ça c'est fort!* as Madame Raymonde would say."

Sir Nicholas eyed his nephew thoughtfully. "So you saw Mrs. O'Toole? I suppose you had some conversation, other than an exchange of expletives."

"Some," Antony admitted. "It wasn't so much what she said, you know, as the language she said it in."

"If that means anything, which I doubt—"

"I think it does, sir. She didn't like questions about Stanley Prior, but she answered them after a little hesitation. She said he lit no lamps for Barbara but was noncommittal about their relationship. She told me Laura Canning was inquisitive, and then seemed to wish she hadn't because she was really evasive about that . . . tried to make out she just meant about Barbara's affairs, and about the shop. But there was something personal, too, and she said another funny thing; that she hadn't seen Laura when she was ill, but 'she would have sought me out when she was ready.'"

"How very helpful!"

"The phrase she used seemed to imply that Laura had some sort of a right to call on her. If she had a hold of any kind over madame—"

"It would, of course, be of the greatest assistance in reinforcing the theory of suicide," said Sir Nicholas ironically.

"She seems to have been very frank with you," remarked Stringer, with a questioning look.

"No. I told you . . . her English is fluent, but she found it easier to lapse into French than hesitate over the answer to an awkward question. I made it pretty clear I didn't understand her very well."

"And was there anything else she found awkward?"

"Only when I wanted to know about Barbara's last day at the shop . . . the day Laura died. That rattled her for some reason." He caught his uncle's eye and added apologetically, "Yes, I know, sir. *Not* helpful. But you did ask me to take a hand, you know."

"An act of incredible folly," said Sir Nicholas. His eyes turned to Derek, who looked resigned and picked up his briefcase and balanced it on his knee. "About tomorrow," said counsel, firmly.

ANTONY WONDERED later if the afternoon had been wasted. They had all gone upstairs to lunch with Jenny (Sir Nicholas having inspected the cold collation his housekeeper had left for him, and pronounced it unfit for human consumption); and afterward— not without misgivings—Antony inserted himself into Derek's car, a Triumph TR4, which had been standing demurely in the square all this while. The trouble was, once Derek got behind the wheel *anything* might happen; he was a dashing and erratic driver, to put it as kindly as possible. On this occasion he seemed preoccupied, and Antony arrived in Roehampton wondering whether this was really preferable to the occasions when he was alert, and seizing every opportunity to circumvent his fellow motorists, whether it existed or not. They went first to see the Newtons, who occupied an imposing residence in Roehampton

Lane, and afterward visited Miss Stuart, who lived in a quaint, attractive little house near the Heath.

The Cannings had occupied the Roehampton flat—which was at the other end of the village, nearer the Portsmouth Road—for nearly five years before the divorce, and both were well known to the Newtons. Mrs. Newton displayed a well-bred ignorance of the cause of their disagreement, though it was evident her sympathies were with Laura. Mr. Newton thought Douglas "not a bad sort of chap" but agreed—with equal vagueness—that Laura was the injured party. Both shook their heads at the mention of Barbara . . . "a great source of anxiety to her sister."

Miss Stuart was more forthright, going so far as to call Barbara a hussy and telling them earnestly that Douglas Canning was too earthy to understand anyone so spiritual as his wife.

"Not precisely what we wanted to hear," said Antony, as they walked down the High Street after they had left her. It was a full day again and already beginning to get dark.

Derek made no direct reply but jingled the loose change in his pocket in a morose way, and after a moment burst out irritably, "What the devil's the matter with you, anyway?"

Antony had been looking over his shoulder, up the almost deserted length of the High Street. He turned back now and grinned apologetically. "Nothing," he said. "Nothing at all." But he sounded uneasy.

"You're giving me the jitters," Derek grumbled.

"I'm sorry, I just thought—"

"The trouble with you," said Stringer flatly, "is that you've got too much imagination."

There seemed to be no good reply to this. Antony resisted the temptation to glance back up the street again, and they walked on in silence until they reached the place where they had left the car.

The house Laura had lived in was about sixty years old, solidly constructed, but with no claims to beauty. There was an imposing porch; the outer door was closed but not locked, and inside two rather narrow doors faced them, each with its brass knocker and letterbox. Derek said, "I'd better tell the old lady; she might think we're burglars," and rang the bell labeled Mills on the left-hand door. It was opened almost immediately by a dark-haired girl of about twenty-three, who thanked him breathlessly for the message and promised to "tell Auntie" who it was upstairs. Derek then produced a large, old-fashioned key, and a moment later the right-hand door swung open. The light from the porch showed them a staircase leading up into obscurity, but Derek pressed the light switch without result. "They might have told me—" he said.

"It'll be better upstairs. I expect we can manage." Antony made an inviting gesture. Stringer hesitated a moment and then led the way up in silence.

The air in the flat was cold and stale and smelled of dust. There were traces, too, that the fingerprint men had been at work. "Uncle Nick only told me what they found—or rather, didn't find—in the kitchen," said Antony, looking around him. "Was there anything else of interest?"

"Not a thing. There were the little girl's prints all over, of course, and Barbara's, and the charwoman's. And the girl we just saw downstairs had left some, too . . . just what you'd expect. If you mean, was there any sign someone else had been here that night . . . there wasn't."

"Let's think about it a minute. Yes, I know it's unlikely," he added, as though his companion had actually made the objection, "but we've got to face the fact that if Barbara didn't do it, and Laura didn't commit suicide, someone else gave her the sedative that night, and a bloody great dose at that. I mean, she was poisoned by giving her extra, wasn't she? Not by putting something into the bottle? So it had to be done by someone who was there."

"I realize that." At the best of times, Derek was never fond of having the obvious explained to him, but Antony was too absorbed to notice the irritation in his friend's tone.

"Well then!" he said. "Suppose someone came and Clare let them in."

"She says she was asleep."

"All right, they had a key. Would Douglas Canning have had one?"

"Barbara said, very definitely, no."

"She has a positive genius for pouring cold water on our efforts. What about Brenda Mills, then? What's she so nervous about?"

Stringer refused to speculate. "She was very positive she didn't give Laura her medicine."

"She might have made a mistake in the dose and then been

afraid to own up. But I didn't mean that ... I hardly think she'd
have gone to the length of letting Barbara be tried for murder. I
meant, she might have let someone in."

"Why?" said Derek.

"Don't be such a killjoy. I'm not saying she did ... I'm saying,
just suppose. *She'd* have opened the downstairs door, and I bet
Laura kept her bedroom door open; she wouldn't want to miss
anything that was going on. Which is her room, Derek?"

"Just behind you, the one on the right."

The door was ajar. Antony pushed it wide and went in. Laura
had loved comfort; if this hadn't been evident from what he had
already heard of her, it would have been obvious now. Even in the
dusk he could see enough to know that it was a very feminine
room ... and now, in its abandoned state, very desolate, the bed
unmade, some powder spilled on the dressing table, and dust
everywhere. He tried to imagine it as it had been, and shivered a
little at the contrast he conjured up. A woman had been alive and
now was dead; and her room was cold and comfortless.

Derek said, impatiently, behind him, "Well, what about it?"

"The easy chair's pulled forward. Barbara said Brenda Mills did
that, but anyway it's upholstered; I doubt if that material would
take fingerprints." (It was a heavy, golden brocade.) "If someone
came, Derek, they needn't have touched anything in here, needn't
have left any sign of their presence."

"It's very unlikely—"

"Yes, I know." But he did not sound despondent. "Someone she
knew well, if she let them pour her medicine."

"There were only Barbara's fingerprints on the bottle."

"That doesn't matter. What shape was it?"

"The usual. Flattish."

"Well then! Use a handkerchief, hold it—awkwardly—by the
two short sides, and Barbara's prints in the usual place needn't be
disturbed at all."

"I don't think—"

"I know you don't." He went quickly out onto the landing again
and stood at the head of the stairs. "That door at the bottom?" he
said.

"Nobody's prints but Barbara's, inside or out."

Antony shot a look at him. "Isn't that rather odd?"

"Not really. I didn't mean the knobs were polished underneath, just smudged. And if you're going to say 'someone with gloves on,'" he added, crossly, "I can only tell you . . . just try and prove it."

"Let's have a look at the rest of the place, then, while we can still see."

He had to go back into Laura's bedroom again, and through the connecting door into the bathroom. More luxury, and the musty smell of stale perfume. Across the landing was a big drawing room. "She must have had this redecorated after Douglas left," said Antony. "No man would stand it." Walls and carpet and upholstery alike were a delicate, pearly gray, relieved only by occasional touches of the palest pink and mauve. There were no pictures, but some china plates carefully arranged, hung on the walls; and all of the same subdued tints. Perhaps the room hadn't been used during Laura's illness; certainly it was unnaturally neat.

Derek said, "Oh, I don't know," vaguely, in answer to his friend's remark, and led the way back across the landing. "They called this the morning room," he said, opening a door opposite the staircase. "When I was here before there were some books, and painting things . . . Clare's, I should think; anyway, they've gone. Then, next to it—" (he went through an archway, into the long, dark corridor beyond) "there's the bedroom Barbara used—the guest room, I suppose—and all her things have been taken away now; then another bathroom, and Clare's room. Her stuff's gone, too. There's nothing to see."

"And beyond that, the kitchen." Antony stood in the doorway and looked curiously round the big, old-fashioned room. It, too, was orderly, though there were cups and plates on a tray on the table, teapot and caddy standing close at hand near the stove, and two crumpled tea towels hanging forlornly near the sink. "And Exhibit A's been moved, of course."

"The glass? It had been put away in the cupboard. A fancy thing, the only one they had like it. Clare bought it, I think . . . that's why her mother liked to use it."

"I see." In the half-light the room seemed vast, cavernlike. Antony strolled across and perched himself on the corner of the table and turned to look at Stringer. "Why are you so sure that Barbara Wentworth is guilty?" he asked.

The abruptness of the question stopped Derek short for a moment; then he moved a little so as to prop himself up in the doorway, and said with an indifference that was badly assumed, "I don't quite see what that has to do with you."

"Don't you?"

"She's pleading not guilty. You know that. But the weight of the evidence—"

"The evidence hasn't convinced Uncle Nick. Not altogether," he added, with reluctant honesty. "That's why I asked you ... what do you know that he doesn't?"

"Nothing at all. How could I?"

"I don't know. But if there's anything you've noticed, Derek ... anything we've missed ... don't you think we ought to know it?"

"Not one thing," said Stringer, violently. "Everything. Every damned thing." He looked across at Antony, whose face he saw now as no more than a blur in the gathering darkness. "I'd give my soul to believe her. But I can't!"

"Don't be so free with your immortal soul," Maitland advised him. "If you stick around, you may regret that bargain."

"She's not being frank with us." He sounded, oddly, as though he were asking for reassurance. "You must see that as well as I do."

"She may be lying like a trooper," said Antony. "I think she is, in spots. But I don't think she killed her sister." He thought, as he spoke, that it was strange he was now so positive ... suddenly, as though his doubts had never been. Somewhere at the back of his mind he connected this certainty with the glimpse he had had of Laura Canning's drawing room; not a very good basis for faith, perhaps, but he had neither time, nor desire, at the moment to study its logic.

Derek made a quick movement, a gesture that might have been one of protest, but he said only, in a strained voice. "Why should she be lying ... if she's nothing to hide?"

"Good lord, a hundred reasons. It makes it more difficult, of course," Antony admitted.

"I should rather say it did!"

"She isn't guilty, Derek."

Stringer laughed shortly. "I never practiced believing six impossible things before breakfast," he remarked.

"Didn't you? It was a defect in your education," said Antony, seriously. "I did ... and I say she's innocent."

"Wishful thinking," said Derek. "You want to believe it."

"D-don't be an idiot. Her l-looks d-don't prove she's a murderess." He saw, with a kind of angry satisfaction, that his companion flinched from the word, as he might have done from a blow.

"I didn't—"

"That's what you're saying, isn't it? That she killed her sister?"

Derek spread his hands helplessly. "Who else?" he said. "Who else?"

Antony got up from the table and went across to stand near the window. "There are difficulties," he said slowly, "about the suicide theory."

"You've noticed that, have you?"

"Irony doesn't really suit you," said Antony reflectively.

"Well, come down to earth a minute, and talk sense." It was Stringer's turn to be angry now. "She's innocent—" his tone was savagely disbelieving "—and we want to prove it. But she gives us no help! She can see well enough where her evidence is leading; every word she says about her return here that night tends to show how unlikely it is that Laura killed herself. And she simply won't deny that there was ill will between them."

"She has a sort of uncompromising honesty," said Antony slowly. "I suppose that's partly the reason I believe her."

Surprisingly, Derek laughed. "I don't think Sir Nicholas finds it a particularly endearing characteristic," he said. "But—look here, Antony—what did you think of her, really?"

"I told you." He sounded weary.

"Yes, but ... as a person ... not just as 'the accused'?"

The room was almost dark now. Antony, turning from the window, could see nothing of his companion's expression. "She's charming," he said carefully. "Intelligent ... courageous—" He paused, as though to contemplate the picture he was presenting. "What's even more to the point, perhaps, her friends are devoted to her."

"It isn't just her looks," said Derek, "it's everything about her." He paused, and then added, with something uncomfortably like desperation, "Antony, what would you do if you thought that Jenny—?"

"The cases are hardly parallel," said Maitland; in spite of himself, the words sounded stiff, unfriendly. "No, but—"

"Well, to begin with, I'd believe what she told me ... even if I didn't. And then I'd do my level best to get her out of it ... whatever trouble she was in."

"The difference is, you *would* believe her," said Derek, "because you know her so well. I don't know Barbara Wentworth at all, but I care quite damnably what happens to her." He paused, and then added resentfully, "I don't know why I'm telling you this."

"Neither do I," said Antony, without much sympathy in his tone. This time Derek's laugh had a note of genuine amusement.

"I'm sorry," he said. "The urge to unload our troubles is a very strong one, isn't it? But the thing is, you see, I'm scared of the whole thing, afraid that whatever we do will make matters worse."

"It can't ... don't you see, it can't? Uncle Nick wouldn't have asked me to interfere if he hadn't known that, as things are, the chances of getting an acquittal are practically nil." Antony spoke with deliberate brutality. Whatever impulse had prompted Derek to confide in him, the only thing he would never forgive would be an open expression of sympathy.

"All right, then. I'll try to forget my feelings and concentrate on the job in hand." There was a bitterness in Derek's tone, but it seemed to be self-directed. "We may as well go, it's too dark to see anything else." He unhitched himself from the doorpost and started to move away down the long corridor, pausing when he reached the landing to let his companion catch up with him. "Don't break your neck down the stairs," he advised. "I seem to be relying on you."

They locked the deserted flat, and went out to the waiting car and drove away in silence. They both had plenty to think about, and for the moment there was a sort of security in the fact that there was no need to talk. After a while, when they stopped for a traffic light in Brompton Road, Antony consulted his watch. "It's too late for tea," he said, a little too elaborately casual. "But you'll come in for a drink, won't you?" It was ridiculous to feel anxious, but the thought came to him that if Derek refused it might mean he was already resenting the confidences he had made. For a moment he thought of Barbara Wentworth with anger, almost with dislike.

But he needn't have worried. Derek said, with an enthusiasm

that sounded quite natural, "Today's great thought. Try and stop me." The light turned green again, and he let in the clutch a little too quickly.

Kempenfeldt Square was almost deserted, and when they drew up outside Sir Nicholas's house on the north side there were only two men in sight, walking toward them from the corner. Derek pocketed the ignition key and paused with his door half open. "By the way," he said, "what were you looking for when we were in Roehampton?"

"Nothing; I mean, it was just a feeling that someone was watching us," said Antony, twisting to see if the road was clear behind him. "Nothing but imagination," he added, firmly.

The answer seemed to satisfy Stringer, who pushed his door wide and scrambled out onto the pavement. The door at the passenger side, which was stiff, delayed Antony for a moment, and while he was still wrestling with the handle he heard the sound of running feet, the thud of a blow, and a grunt of pain from the other side of the car. He was out then in an instant, and perhaps some instinct forbade him to slam the door. He came round the front of the car in a silent rush toward the tangle of figures on the pavement. There wasn't any time to consider the niceties of the situation. He brought down his left hand viciously on the nearest man's neck, and saw him topple soundlessly. At almost the same instant Derek, whose hat had fallen off in the struggle, went down more slowly onto his knees, and then sprawled sideways on the ground. The man who had hit him hesitated, with a look for his fallen comrade; then he flung his weapon with a theatrical and despairing gesture right into Antony's face and made off as fast as he could, toward the corner.

The thing that hit him was both hard and pliant, and it rocked Antony back on his heels for a moment. By then, the second man was passing out of sight. He checked the instinct to give chase; the bodies on the pavement seemed of more immediate concern. He was pretty sure the man he had hit wouldn't come round in a hurry; but he only hoped Derek hadn't been badly hurt.

6

HE WASN'T EVEN UNCONSCIOUS very long, and Dr. Prescott—responding with commendable speed to the note of urgency in Jenny's summons—was reassuringly cheerful. Mrs. Stokes arrived from the nether regions, frankly enjoying the fuss. A taciturn constable possessed himself of the weapons—two long canvas tubes, sand-filled—arranged the removal of the remaining assailant and took statements, impartially, from everyone in sight.

"With you, Antony, was he?" asked the doctor, with an eloquent jerk of the head in Stringer's direction. "He should choose his companions more carefully." He looked around, obviously contemplating some indiscretion; but Jenny, who was bathing the lump on the victim's head, was only a few feet away. "Ah, well," said Dr. Prescott, "rest's the thing. Rest, and perhaps a couple of aspirin tablets. Fit as a fiddle in a couple of days," he assured the patient. Derek scowled at him, but later consented—after only a little persuasion—to spend the evening with his friends, and the night in Sir Nicholas's spare bedroom. Antony breathed a silent prayer of thankfulness that Gibbs was absent, and went away to raid his uncle's supply of spirits before he went upstairs. Come to think of it, it was lucky Uncle Nick was out, too. He wasn't in the mood for the explanations he felt would be expected; and was, besides, completely bewildered himself at the turn events had taken.

He had intended to put in the whole of the next day in court, but a summons from Scotland Yard delayed him. Detective-Inspector Sykes would be much obliged . . . .

"Let me talk to him," said Antony, who was just finishing his breakfast. There was a few minutes' delay while the inspector was located, and then he heard the deep voice that so often seemed to have an undercurrent of amusement.

"Good morning, Mr. Maitland."

"Look here, what's all this about?"

"That's just what I want to find out. There's a report on my desk—"

"Yes, I know. But I told your chaps all about it." There was a pause, and he added unkindly, "If you want to inquire after my health, don't bother. It wasn't I who was attacked, you know."

"All the same," said Sykes. There was a note of inflexibility in his voice. Antony turned his head and pulled a face at Jenny, who was watching him over the rim of her coffee cup. "If it's not convenient for you to come to the Yard, Mr. Maitland, I'll gladly come to you."

Antony reflected. It would be easier to see the detective in chambers, but old Mr. Mallory would probably be affronted, and he had the most ingenious ways of making his displeasure felt. "Never mind," he said, "I'll come to you . . . if I must." But he did not sound cordial, and the receiver went down with something of a snap.

Jenny was pouring him another cup of coffee. "I don't suppose he'll keep you long," she said.

"It isn't that." He eyed the telephone unlovingly. "Uncle Nick's in a bad enough mood already."

"I don't see . . . I mean, it wasn't really anything to do with you, was it?" said Jenny.

"Of course it wasn't." But his doubtful tone ruined the effect of the reassurance. He caught her eye, and added more confidently: "Honestly, love, I don't see how it could have been. But you heard what Dr. Prescott said . . . and now Sykes . . . oh, well!" He drank some of the coffee and set down the cup with a clatter. "I wonder how Derek's feeling this morning," he said. "He made up his mind he was going to court, but I hope he can get his wig on."

"At least, if he can, the lump on his head won't show." Jenny was eyeing her husband critically. "You look awful, darling," she told him; and in this she did not exaggerate, for he had a black eye, and his face was bruised where the sandbag had hit him.

Detective-Inspector Sykes was a square-built man, with an admirable placidity of temperament, and a north-country broadness of speech that his long sojourn in London had done nothing to soften. He greeted Antony as an old friend, ignored the rather grudging tone of his responses, and gave him a searching look, but made no more open comment on his appearance. "A nasty business," he remarked, as he settled himself again behind the wide, untidy desk.

"But not, I should have thought, your concern," said Antony, sourly. He couldn't help it; police inquiries—the need to answer questions and look as if you liked it—always irked him.

"You'd be surprised, Mr. Maitland ... or perhaps you wouldn't," Sykes corrected himself. "And as to this affair, I admit I'm curious. Speaking unofficially ... what are you up to?"

Antony smiled at him. He never could maintain a grudge for long, and now he didn't know whether to be more amused by the query or annoyed by it. Perhaps the latter emotion predominated; at any rate, his reply was not altogether without malice. "Nothing at all, Inspector," he said, airily. And knew as he spoke that Sykes wasn't going to believe him.

"You've no idea," the detective persisted, "why this attack should have been made?"

"Shouldn't that question be addressed to Stringer? He was the one they jumped on, you know; and as he was getting out of his own car, too."

"They wouldn't have laid in wait for him in Kempenfeldt Square," Sykes pointed out.

"Then I suppose it was armed robbery; but it didn't look like it to me," Antony admitted.

"Nor to anyone else. So that's why I'm asking," said the inspector earnestly, "who had a motive for attacking you?" He glanced down at the papers on his desk. "Mr. Stringer's car, which is a distinctive model, was parked outside your house from eleven-thirty in the morning until you went out with him at about two o'clock," he went on. "So a stranger might have been forgiven for thinking it yours, and expecting you to get out of the driver's seat. Someone who didn't know you by sight, and wanted to catch you coming home after dark."

"A stranger wouldn't have had a grudge against me," said Antony. He sounded stubborn, and Sykes gave him a grim look.

"I don't know why I bother," he remarked, not quite in his usual level tone.

"Either you're an incurable optimist or a hopeless cynic," Antony suggested. "But you misjudge me, Inspector. I'm confused myself, but I was trying to be helpful."

"Were you, Mr. Maitland? Then tell me, has your work ever

brought you into contact with any of the racetrack gangs?"

"Racetrack—?" said Antony, in obvious bewilderment. And then, "Oh, I see. The chap I hit."

"Name of Badger," Sykes told him. "His real name, apparently. He has a bad reputation for violence, a couple of convictions. Not a brain though, just carrying out orders ... strong-arm stuff."

Antony was thinking this out. "Then I suppose we can consider ourselves lucky it wasn't razors," he said. "But I haven't the remotest idea—really, Inspector!—of any connection."

"No case you were involved in? It might have been some time ago."

"There was one, at Liverpool Assizes, in 1956 ... I think," said Antony doubtfully. "Halloran went up on a special, and I got roped in, too; I can't remember why. He led me in quite a few cases about then."

"An aggrieved client?" Sykes suggested.

"I don't think ... I haven't the faintest idea what he was called, but he was a nice little chap, a clerk with one of the big bookmakers. I can't remember the details offhand; in fact, I only remember it at all because I was rather upset about it at the time."

"Why?"

"Because I felt the verdicts were unfair. There were six or seven defendants ... rather a sophisticated swindle ... our chap had been an essential part of it, they had to have someone on the inside, but he swore he'd acted under threat of violence, and I believed him."

"Did Mr. Halloran believe him too?" asked Sykes, dryly. Antony grinned at him.

"As a matter of fact, I think he did."

"Perhaps one of the other men thought you'd treated him unfairly in saving your client."

"I told you, it was seven years ago. Anyway, it couldn't have been like that, that's what worried me at the time. Our chap got four years, while the one who'd obviously masterminded the whole thing was acquitted. And don't tell me our client bore a grudge because we didn't get him off; he was almost pathetically grateful for what Halloran had tried to do."

"So we're back where we started. If you haven't any racing connections, who wanted you beaten up?"

"Oh, w-what's the use?" There had been a skepticism in the

detective's voice, which ruffled his companion's already uncertain temper. "You've got—what's his name, Badger?—in custody, haven't you? What's he got to say for himself?"

It was Sykes's turn to smile, which he managed to do without lessening the sedateness of his demeanor. "The poor fellow's an innocent bystander," he declared solemnly. "He saw the attack, and was just going to the rescue when a second desperado went for him from the rear."

Antony eyed him speechlessly for a moment. "He didn't explain how he happened to be carrying an offensive weapon, I suppose." he said at last. "He hit Derek first, you know, only he dodged and took the blow on his shoulder; and then the other chap came up from behind."

"He's never seen such a thing before," said Sykes; and at this point he was obviously enjoying himself. "Nor he wouldn't have known what it was for ... not unless we'd told him."

"I suppose *I* dropped it," suggested Antony, amused.

"That seems to be the general idea. However, the doctor bears out your story of the way you hit him." This was evidently said with intent to annoy, but there was a speculative look in his eye.

"Well, if he's denying everything, obviously he won't tell you who his accomplice was, or who hired them."

"Obviously not. Do you think there's any chance you might be able to identify—"

"I could try, of course. But I'm a bit doubtful ... the light wasn't good, you know."

"Just a few photographs ... Badger's known associates," said Sykes, persuasively.

"Well of course—" Antony was frowning over the suggestion; more of his morning gone, but he couldn't very well refuse.

"Thank you, Mr. Maitland. But you still haven't told me—" said Sykes; and watched his visitor's expression become even more forbidding.

"If you're back at the motive again—" said Antony, furiously.

"Let's get at it another way. Your professional engagements—?"

"My last client was a free-lance writer who'd been rather indiscreet," said Maitland. "And the matter was settled out of court, so I don't suppose either side felt particularly aggrieved by the result."

"Sir Nicholas," said Sykes, making an uncharacteristically impatient gesture—perhaps he was symbolically throwing caution to the winds. "Sir Nicholas has been briefed for the defense in the Wentworth trial." And this was the detective's real interest in the attack, Antony realized, the thing that brought it—just possibly—within his own field of activities.

"I'm taking a hand behind the scenes," he admitted. "If that's what you want to know."

"I was wondering."

"If I thought the two things were connected I'd tell you. Why shouldn't I?"

If Sykes thought, "sheer perversity," he didn't say so. He maintained his benign expression. "No reason at all, Mr. Maitland. But I can't help feeling you might think of half a dozen," he said.

"Hopelessly cynical. I *said* so," remarked Antony, gloomily.

"Well, if you can't help me, you can't. I was just wondering," said Sykes, with the air of one laying his cards on the table, "whether any of the questions you'd been asking—"

"I'm often tactless, Inspector, but ... no, honestly, this time I don't see how there can be a connection." I wish I did, he thought; it would mean, for sure, there was something to uncover after all. "Anyway," he added, "the case is closed—isn't it?—so far as you're concerned."

"That's right." Sykes got up as he spoke, and came around the desk. "But—speaking unofficially, Mr. Maitland—" for my own good, thought Antony, with renewed irritation "—are the defense calling Douglas Canning?"

"No, they're not." If his tone was guarded it was because the question was so unexpected.

"Well ... talk to him," said Sykes. "And for goodness' sake, lad, don't tell anyone I said so." He urged his visitor toward the door, as though only by getting him out of the room quickly could he be saved from further indiscretion.

MR. JUSTICE CARRUTHERS was a small man who looked like an intelligent bloodhound. He was being bored by the medical evidence, about which there seemed to be no argument; the poor woman was dead, and that was all there was to it. And it wasn't up to the doctors to say who had administered the dose of sedative that killed her.

But Lamb was always thorough, and it wouldn't do to ask the jury to take anything for granted. And presently Harding would rouse himself from what seemed to be a coma and take a hand in the affair. There was usually a surprise or two in store when he appeared for the defense.

Meanwhile, the newspapers needed no further material to turn the affair into a sensation— which they had done very effectively, thought the judge, letting his eyes rest consideringly for a moment on the crowd in the public gallery. All murder victims were "beautiful," of course, if they were women and even fairly young; and in this case, most likely, the description had been accurate. So there was the headline ready-made: "Beautiful young divorcee," and later the prisoner's picture to embellish their columns still further. And no doubt at all in this case whether the caption "Beautiful model" was deserved. Since the dock was directly opposite the bench he was able to study the accused woman covertly from time to time without the discourtesy of an open stare; an interesting face, he thought . . . if she killed her sister, I hope we're going to be told why.

The doctor who had prescribed Mrs. Canning's sedative was droning on about her illness, about her medical background. A movement in the doorway caught the judge's attention in time for him to see a tall figure come down the room and slip into the first vacant seat found on the barristers' benches. Carruthers's expression never varied, but he was aware of a quickening of interest. Maitland hadn't been briefed for the defense, he knew that well enough; so if he were taking a hand, it might well be that the word "sensational" as applied to the trial wouldn't turn out to be just a piece of fantasy on the part of the press.

At this point Sir Nicholas woke up, either because some sixth sense had warned him the examination-in-chief was coming to an end or because he guessed the slight commotion behind him was due to his nephew's arrival. At any rate, he turned his head and darted a look at the newcomer that was anything but welcoming. The judge concealed his amusement. There were some among his colleagues who disapproved of Maitland, but for his part he liked him well enough and found his lack of conformity refreshing. Not that there was anything the severest critic could complain of in his courtroom manner, even if his present appearance was a little unorthodox.

Antony, encountering a look from his uncle that ought to have withered him, and would certainly have caused a degree of soul-searching if he hadn't known perfectly well what was wrong, subsided decorously onto a seat next to his learned friend Mr. Porterhouse and wondered to how many more people he would have to explain the black eye before the end of the day. It was ironical that Derek—who must have a beast of a headache this morning—should be the one who showed no signs of the conflict.

He didn't think he'd missed much; there was a stunned feeling about the court that argued unmistakably that here was a witness who had gone on too long. A tall, portly man, impeccably dressed ... "Dead woman's doctor," whispered Porterhouse helpfully beside him. Only Sir Gerald Lamb was taking an interest now, and he didn't seem to be enjoying it. A moment later he had thanked the witness and seated himself, and Sir Nicholas was on his feet.

"Mrs. Canning had been suffering from influenza," he remarked.

"That is quite correct."

"And this sedative which you prescribed ... would that be something you normally recommend for a patient who is convalescent after an attack of influenza?"

"I hoped I had made it clear that it was not a normal part of the treatment."

"You must forgive my ignorance, Doctor. Something in Mrs. Canning's condition, then, made it advisable that she should take a sedative?"

"Yes."

"Her physical condition?"

"Not precisely."

"Her mental condition, then?"

"To take a sedative at night is not uncommon," said the witness stiffly.

"Not at all. But insomnia ... you are telling us that Mrs. Canning suffered from insomnia?"

"Yes."

"And as there was no physical reason to account for it, we can take it that her mental condition was responsible?"

"Her state of mind. Yes." He sounded reluctant. "In these cases it is not at all easy to determine—"

"We need not delve too deeply into metaphysics," Sir Nicholas assured him. "We have established—have we not?—that Mrs. Canning was in the habit of taking a sleeping drug. Now, what would you say was the reason for the state of mind that made it necessary? Was she worried, for instance?"

"Sometimes."

"Do you think she had reason to be worried?"

"I cannot say."

"She did not confide in you?"

"No."

"Would you say she was unduly given to worrying ... that things preyed on her mind to an abnormal extent?"

"Not at all." The witness paused there, but as Sir Nicholas opened his mouth for the next question was inspired to add, "She was a very sensitive person."

"She felt things more deeply than most of us do. Is that what you mean?" Sir Nicholas glanced at counsel for the prosecution, who was listening intently, and appeared to be sunk in gloom.

"Yes, certainly."

"And so was in need of sedation. Tell me, Doctor, how did this sensitivity of her manifest itself?"

"I think I know what I'm talking about," said the witness, affronted.

"Was she nervous ... hysterical—?"

"I have attended her when she was in a very nervous state."

"Depressed? Crying?"

"On occasions, yes."

"And it was to avoid these outbursts that you prescribed the sedative?"

"I suppose that is one way of putting it." But his agreement was grudging.

"I am here to be informed, Doctor. How, then, would you express the matter?"

"Well, I ... life is not easy for a woman alone."

"A sensitive woman?"

"I do not think there was anything unusual in her needing this help."

"So when you say she did not worry unduly, you mean not unduly for someone in a disturbed mental state."

"That is not what I said," protested the witness, with truth.

"I am getting a little tired of the word 'sensitive,'" said Sir Nicholas tartly.

Counsel for the prosecution came halfway to his feet and said, "M'lud!" It was more a groan than a protest.

"I think, perhaps, if you were to frame a question, Sir Nicholas—"

"I shall be happy to do so, m'lud." No one else, Antony thought, would have noticed the slight self-satisfaction that to him was apparent in his uncle's voice. Sir Nicholas turned to the witness and said, smoothly, "Did you ever consider the possibility that Mrs. Canning would take her own life?"

"Never for a moment."

"So really you cannot speak to its likelihood," said Sir Nicholas regretfully, "if you never gave the matter any thought." And sat down quickly, before the doctor could spoil his effect by any more explanations.

Antony borrowed a pencil from his neighbor and started to draw a crocodile on the back of an envelope. He didn't think it was a very good likeness, but at least you could see the tears.

The remaining medical witness was the doctor who had attended the Wentworth family in Southbourne, and Lamb's examination of him didn't leave the defense with much room for maneuver. The Solicitor-General knew now the lines on which the prisoner's counsel were fighting, and inevitably the emphasis of his questions altered, discounting in advance—as far as possible—the points that would be made in cross-examination.

Sir Gerald Lamb was a man of middle height, with straight, thick hair, a scholarly face, and pince-nez perched on an aristocratic nose. He had an odd way of carrying his shoulders, so that he looked like nothing so much as a large, melancholy bird, hunched against the wind. Antony, listening to him now with interest and appreciation, couldn't help but admire the dexterity with which he was spiking Sir Nicholas's guns.

The old doctor from Southbourne was inclined to be sentimental over his former patients. "Two lovely girls," he said, and carefully avoided looking at the woman in the dock. But he had seen little of Barbara, beyond attending her for the usual childish ailments; "always so healthy and high-spirited," he told them, and it was odd how the words seemed to become a condemnation. He hadn't liked Barbara, but he couldn't say enough about Laura, who was shy and delicate and had often needed his services. But there had been nothing to indicate any abnormality of mind ... oh, no, indeed. As a child she had always had the highest principles ... the very idea that she might have committed suicide was a wicked suggestion ....

Sir Nicholas declined to cross-examine with a sad, saintlike smile, which somehow contrived to suggest that he was doing the court a favor. Which, indeed, the jury may have felt, as the judge promptly adjourned for the luncheon recess.

Across a corner table at Astroff's Restaurant, Sir Nicholas regarded his companions with disfavor. He had, of course, alternative subjects for recrimination, and Antony had been taking a bet with himself which would be raised first. In the event his uncle chose to combine the two.

"Since apparently you cannot undertake the simplest mission without getting into a brawl," he said caustically, "I suppose I shouldn't have been surprised when Jenny informed me you had been requested to go to Scotland Yard."

"It wasn't really a brawl, Uncle Nick. Derek was attacked and I—"

"Rushed heroically to the rescue. I don't want to hear about that," said Sir Nicholas repressively. "Besides which, I gather from Prescott you made use of some rather rough and ready methods. Something you learned from that gang of thugs in Whitehall, I presume."

This didn't seem to be the time to protest at this description of his wartime colleagues. "Rough, but effective," he agreed.

"And will look well in the papers." He gave his nephew ample time to digest this, as the waiter arrived at that moment and he ordered, arbitrarily, for the three of them. Then, "What did Sykes want?" he asked, abruptly.

"The usual, sir. He thinks I know something he doesn't."

"About the Wentworth affair?"

"Yes. But he was jumping to conclusions ... don't you think?"

"I don't know," said Sir Nicholas. He sounded suddenly worried and uncertain, but Derek put in eagerly:

"Did you tell him you thought someone was following us in Roehampton?"

"There was nothing to tell. It was only a feeling; I didn't see anybody."

"All the same, if there was someone there—"

"It means whoever carried out the attack was pretty well organized ... that's all. It doesn't connect it in any way with Barbara Wentworth."

"But if that was why ... because someone didn't like you asking questions—"

"*If,*" said Antony, crossly. "I'd hardly begun, you know. Who are you suggesting took umbrage ... Jill, or Dorothy, or madame?" But he smiled as another thought struck him. "It might just as well have been Bellerby ... now there's a thought, Uncle Nick! He isn't very pleased with me."

"Why not?" asked Derek. Sir Nicholas said nothing but compressed his lips in an ominous way.

"Oh ... well!" Antony was vague. "And to get back to Sykes, sir," he added—which was really the last thing he wanted to do— "he says the chap they've got in custody is a racetrack tough, which I don't find illuminating. And if we ever do find anything out about Laura Canning's death, after days of patient endeavor, I'll never convince him I didn't have some inside information all the time." He took advantage of the waiter's return to ask Derek how his head was feeling; and was grateful that Sir Nicholas, seizing instead on this secondary grievance, did not return to the subject of the police.

"He is here," said Sir Nicholas, "in direct defiance of the doctor's wishes—"

The theme lasted him until the main course was served, at which time he permitted himself to be diverted by an ingenious question from Stringer about a case of arson which had been reported in the Sunday newspapers. Antony concentrated on the sweetbreads his uncle had ordered; they were a delicacy to which he was not partial.

7

RETURNING TO COURT after the recess, Antony found a seat nearer the center of things. Mr. Bellerby greeted him coldly but then relented sufficiently—either from sympathy or curiosity—to ask him (for a change) where he'd got that black eye. Antony, recognizing an *amende* when he saw it, repressed his desire to answer facetiously and was rewarded when his account of the engagement had the effect of turning the solicitor's commiserating attention on Derek. He was still expressing his horror when Mr. Justice Carruthers took his place on the bench.

There was a livelier feeling in the air this afternoon; it was a relief to be through with the medical evidence, and besides, the worst of Monday was over. The exception, of course, was counsel for the prosecution, whose perpetual gloom nothing seemed to disturb. And the witness . . . .

Mrs. Mills owned the house in Roehampton where Laura Canning had died, and herself occupied the ground-floor apartment. Watching her as she answered Sir Gerald's questions, Antony thought he now knew exactly what the phrase "distressed gentlewoman" really meant. She was painfully refined, and she looked like something out of one of the less cheerful Russian novels.

Yes, Mrs. Canning had lived in the flat above her for over eight years. At first with her husband, and of course the little girl. Such a nice couple she had thought them, and so well recommended; Mrs. Canning had always shown herself a perfect lady, and even after the divorce—in *all* the circumstances, you know—she had had no qualms about her staying on as tenant. No, she knew nothing about her circle of friends; she hoped she was never one to interfere, and each apartment was completely self-contained, with separate front doors. But she had visited dear Mrs. Canning almost every day during her illness and would have been glad to do more if Miss Wentworth hadn't insisted on coming to stay. On the day of her death Mrs. Canning had been cheerful and looking forward to getting up at the weekend. She didn't know of any visitors that evening; she thought she would have heard because the paneling that enclosed the staircase wasn't really very thick. And Miss Wentworth came in quite early; she couldn't tell the time for sure because she had been reading, but it wasn't very long after Brenda came down. She didn't know Miss Wentworth well; she didn't often visit her sister, which made it all the more strange . . . .

At this point counsel for the defense came to his feet with a look of shocked incredulity. But as Sir Gerald Lamb was already thanking his witness, the protest he was framing remained unuttered.

Sir Nicholas was almost foiled at the outset when his question as to the number of her brothers and sisters brought the prim reply that she was an only child. Rallying, he said sympathetically, "Then you cannot know, madam, how members of a family— perhaps without very much in common— will come together, will lend a helping hand in times of trouble.

"Mrs. Canning wasn't in any trouble," the witness pointed out.

"In times of sickness," counsel amended. "It wasn't so very strange, really, that Miss Wentworth should want to be with her sister."

"Perhaps it wasn't."

"Now, you have told us you saw Mrs. Canning the day she died. What time was that?"

"Round about teatime. The charwoman was there during the day, you see— Mrs. Paley, she's a very good sort of woman— but it does no harm just to see if everything's been done, with dear Mrs. Canning being in bed, and Miss Wentworth not really used to domestic matters, I suppose." Counsel opened his mouth, but the flood went on unabated. "Besides, at that time Clare would be coming home from school, though she was a little late that evening, as I remember, and Mrs. Paley would have the kettle on, so I could enjoy a cup of tea with Mrs. Canning and be sure everything was nice for her."

There was a pause; perhaps Sir Nicholas was afraid of being swept away on another tide of information. "Have you ever had influenza, madam?" he inquired cautiously.

"Oh, yes, indeed. I don't think a winter passes . . . and sometimes more than once. So debilitating," she said.

"Er—yes. And depressing—wouldn't you say?—especially when you reach convalescence."

"Very depressing. I know once I—"

"But Mrs. Canning was cheerful that day?"

"She was still weak. But looking forward to getting up."

"And putting a brave front on her depression?"

"That describes it very well."

"And that evening . . . you heard Miss Wentworth come in?"

"Brenda came down after Clare went to bed. Later I heard someone running up the stairs."

"Could that have been as late as ten-fifteen?"

"I didn't really notice . . . no, of course, it couldn't," she said, triumphantly. "It must have been before a quarter to ten."

"You were reading," he reminded her.

"Until a quarter to ten. I was in the front room with the door open. Then I went down to the kitchen to make some cocoa, and I wouldn't have heard if a regiment had gone upstairs."

"Was your niece still in the front room?"

"Brenda? Oh, no, she had already gone to bed. She thought she might be starting a cold, so I said I'd take her a hot drink."

It was surprising how long Mrs. Mills's evidence took, though it wasn't particularly rewarding for either side. "Summat and nowt," thought Antony to himself—his attention had wandered, and he had been meditating on his interview with Inspector Sykes. Sir Nicholas sat down and closed his eyes. "You can have the niece," he said to Derek Stringer. "If there's any resemblance—"

There wasn't. Brenda Mills gave her evidence with a sort of breathless anxiety and showed no disposition at all to let her answers run away with her. She repeated, with one significant addition, what her aunt had said, but in a colorless way, and with no intrusion of her own opinions. The afternoon grew darker outside, and Antony's thoughts drifted far away from the courtroom; he was making a mental inventory of facts, but didn't get very far with it . . . it was far more intriguing to speculate on Douglas Canning, and what Sykes's rather cryptic hints had meant.

But some instinct for essentials brought him back to the trial just as Stringer was asking, "You went up to Mrs. Canning's flat about eight o'clock the night she died?"

"Yes."

"Just before Miss Wentworth went out?"

"A few minutes before."

"What did you do then?"

"I'd brought my knitting."

"So you sat and talked with Mrs. Canning?"

"Part of the time."

"What else did you do?"

"Clare was doing her homework, you see. She was in the little room they call the morning room. And sometimes Mrs. Canning would say, 'Surely she's finished by now,' or something like that. And then I would go and look."

"How did Mrs. Canning seem?"

"Oh, just as usual, really. Except for being in bed."

"And what was 'just as usual'?" (Derek was really showing a commendable patience.)

"Quiet. Not very much to say."

"A little 'down' after her illness?"

"I don't know. She was always like that."

"Did Clare finish her homework?"

"Yes, just before nine o'clock. Mrs. Canning thought she looked tired and said she should go to bed straight away, and asked me to get her a glass of milk. So I did."

"The milk was for the little girl?"

"Yes."

"Nothing for Mrs. Canning?"

"Oh, no."

"So Clare went to bed, and you went back to Mrs. Canning's room?"

"Yes. And she asked if Clare was all right, and I told her. And then she said she was feeling very sleepy, and wouldn't I like to go because she was sure Barbara would be home early. I thought perhaps I ought to stay, but she sort of insisted."

"I see. Now, Miss Mills, did she ask you to give her her medicine before you left?"

"No. Oh, no."

"She was drowsy, you say. Perhaps she had taken it already."

"No, she hadn't."

"You have described the bedside table: that there was a bottle of medicine, and a glass, and an old-fashioned water bottle."

"The glass had some flowers painted on it."

"Everything to Mrs. Canning's hand, so that she could help herself?"

"Well ... yes."

"Perhaps she had taken the sedative while you were in the kitchen."

"Oh, no, I remember quite well before I left ... the glass was still on the bedside table, and it hadn't been used."

"Are you sure it was then you noticed it? Immediately before you left?"

"Quite sure. Or I'd have washed the glass out."

"Of course, you would do that instinctively. Might you not have done so, and forgotten?"

"I'm quite sure I didn't. Quite, quite sure." And though she became even more worried and apologetic when Stringer pressed his questions, she stuck to her denial.

Mrs. Paley, who had been willing to "oblige" Laura Canning from time to time, was another voluble witness who had very little that was material to add. Here a little and there a little, said Antony to himself; but that was Lamb all over ... careful, and so thorough it drove you mad. But Sir Gerald seemed to feel no satisfaction in a job well done; his depression remained as profound as ever.

Mrs. Canning, said the witness, had been an angel from heaven, if ever there was one. (Derek looked around and grimaced at Antony, at this unwelcome confirmation of what he had said.) Never a cross word, said Mrs. Paley, and that grateful ... anything you could do, it was a real pleasure. As she spoke, Barbara Wentworth turned slowly and watched her, a movement which caught Antony's attention, as it marked the first sign of interest she had shown in the proceedings that day. He leaned forward and hissed in Derek's ear, "The lady doth protest too much." Stringer nodded violently but did not again look round.

So she'd been glad, said Mrs. Paley, to arrange to stay the full day when Miss Wentworth asked her to. Not at weekends, of course, and not in the evenings. But Miss Wentworth never kept her waiting, she would say that, and always a word of apology if she did. As for the day Mrs. Canning died, she remembered it vividly and described it in detail. And then when she arrived next morning, to find the poor lamb dead ....

"We shall be obliged to you, Mrs. Paley, if you will describe to us what happened," said counsel for the prosecution, in tones of despair. (Poor lamb, thought Antony; but did anyone ever make jocular remarks to Sir Gerald, who ought, by rights, to have been called Jeremiah?)

"I let myself in, and when I got upstairs Miss Wentworth was just coming out of the bathroom. She had her dressing gown on. 'Oh, Mrs. Paley,' she says, 'I've got the kettle on; but I overslept and I haven't had time to make my sister's breakfast.' 'That's all right, miss,' I say, thinking I'd do it right away and give her a cup of tea, if she liked, before she went out. 'And how does she find herself this morning?' I asks, meaning Mrs. Canning. And she says she hasn't been in yet to see."

"What time was this, Mrs. Paley?"

"Close on eight o'clock. Well, about ten to, I suppose."

"And then?"

"Miss Wentworth went into Miss Clare's room, and I heard them talking but I couldn't hear what was said. And I went into the kitchen, and there was the kettle, boiling its head off. So I turned down the gas and went back to Mrs. Canning's room to ask what she'd fancy—she'd been that pernickety, you wouldn't believe—and when I'd pulled the curtains there she was ... dead!"

Naturally, they weren't to get away without a description of her emotions, and after that the details of the room as she found it took some time. And no use trying to shake her on any point, when their client agreed with every word she said and was obviously ready—not to say determined—to confirm this agreement as soon as she got the chance. So there was nothing for the defense to do but go on hitting the same old nail on the head; and even if we succeed in making them believe in this "postinfluenzal depression," thought Antony, almost as hopelessly as Sir Gerald himself might have done, we can't get round the question ... who took away the glass? But Derek was still trying to do so when the court adjourned n the late afternoon.

Mr. Bellerby had held Stringer back in anxious consultation. Antony, a little at a loss in his role of supernumerary, began to drift across the courtroom in his uncle's wake. Near the door an attendant came up to Sir Nicholas with a note. "You may find it's been a little delayed, sir. The address—"

There was careful printing on the envelope: "Miss Barbara Wentworth's lawyer, Old Bailey, London." Inside was a single sheet of notepaper, and the message was printed in a sprawling, childish hand, the letters growing bigger and bigger as they crossed the sheet. Sir Nicholas read, and handed it to his nephew in silence.

"she didn't   she didn't   she didn't"
the message protested.

"Clare?" said Antony.

"I suppose so. Poor child," sighed Sir Nicholas. He held out a hand for the paper and folded it back into its envelope. "If you see her, Antony, be kind to her," he said.

"I'm not a m-monster," said Antony, crossly. But much later he was to remember that conversation, as though they had been standing quietly isolated in the clatter of the rapidly emptying courtroom, and each word had a significance of which they were then only half-aware.

DOUGLAS CANNING was living in Wood Green now, with his second wife and his daughter. Antony telephoned from chambers and arranged to see him after dinner, but declined Derek's offer to accompany him. Stringer then admitted to a headache—which was sufficiently obvious from his heavy-eyed appearance—and went off home, promising himself an early night. Sir Nicholas was entertaining that evening and needed Jenny as hostess, so Antony struggled through dinner with a judge's widow (deaf) on one side of him and a severe-looking lady who appeared to be a devotee of the newest religion on the other. The excuses he made when the meal was over were genuine enough but only just escaped betraying his relief.

It was colder tonight, and the fog seemed to have lifted a little. It would have been nice to have Derek's company and still better to have his services as a chauffeur, in spite of that being a somewhat nerve-racking experience. But it was so long since the wartime injury to his shoulder had resulted in Antony's giving up driving that he took the inconvenience for granted by now and made for the nearest tube station philosophically enough.

The Cannings lived in a newish, rather dreary-looking house on an estate that was still being developed. Inside, the furnishings were equally undistinguished, but the sitting room into which Douglas conducted him was warm and cheerful. Canning was a sandy-haired, thin-faced man, with an air of anxiety about him, and when he said, "This is my wife. Emmie, this is Mr. Maitland," Antony felt he had no difficulty in identifying the source of the room's comfort and was even ready to forgive her the china "bunnies" on the mantelpiece for the friendliness of her greeting. Emily Canning was a small woman with a comfortable figure and a round face rather reminiscent of a Dutch doll. The likeness was heightened by her straight, fair hair, which she wore rather short.

"It's a cold night," she said. "Come and sit here, near the fire." Antony obeyed her; he thought afterward that it was like being borne along on a tide of warm treacle . . . oddly, a rather pleasant sensation. She took the chair opposite him and eyed him with unconcealed curiosity. "If you can help Barbara, Douglas will be ever so grateful to you," she told him.

Douglas pulled up a chair and seated himself, not leaning back. "She's quite right," he said. "But I've talked to the solicitor, of course, and I don't think it was very helpful."

"Well, you see—" Antony thought, as he spoke, of the two girls to whom he had made a similar explanation on Saturday; "a forlorn hope," Dorothy had said, and that just about described it. But as Douglas seemed to be concerned for his sister-in-law, he had to find something more heartening to say. "So I hoped you could fill in some of the details for me about . . . Laura," he concluded. (After all, he couldn't go on referring to "the first Mrs. Canning" all the evening.) "What was she like . . . and her friends . . . and so on."

To his relief, Emmie got up in a purposeful way. "I shall go and make coffee," she said. "Then you can be comfortable." He hadn't suspected her of so much tact.

For a moment Douglas remained looking at the door through which his wife had disappeared. Then he turned back to Antony and smiled for the first time so that some of the haggardness disappeared from his face, and he immediately looked younger. "Ten minutes, about," he said. "Where do you want to begin?"

"When you first met the Wentworths. How did you meet Laura?"

"I went down to Southbourne for a holiday and joined the tennis club she belonged to as a guest member. After that I used to go down when I could, and in between we wrote to each other. And the next year we were married. She was twenty then."

"Was she as beautiful as her sister?" The other man's reminiscent tone was an encouragement to his questions.

"Barbara was just a kid, nice looking, of course, but nothing out of the way. As for Laura, I suppose pretty would describe her better. Very pretty."

"What was she like?"

"Gentle ... well-mannered. Very popular with her friends. Nice to her parents."

"And Barbara?"

"A little fiend." He smiled as he spoke. "Well, not too little, really; overgrown and leggy. But definitely a fiend."

"And so you and Laura were married?"

"Yes. We lived in Putney at first, down by the river; I've always worked in London, you know. And then we moved to Roehampton ... well, things were easier financially after her parents died."

"Did it strike you as odd, the way things were left?"

"Well, yes and no. I knew they were hurt when Barbara came to London."

"But Laura would always have been ready to help her sister?"

Douglas hesitated, and then said, choosing his words with care, "If Barbara had asked her, she'd have helped her ... at a price."

"I see. You described your first wife a moment ago. Was that ... just an illusion?"

"Not really. It was only that ... there was another side to her, you see." He spoke unwillingly, but then, surprisingly, he smiled. "You ask the most damnable questions," he said.

"I'm afraid so." He was beginning to like Douglas Canning; but he thought his reticences even more revealing than his apparent willingness to talk. "This 'other side,' now?" he said, persuasively.

"She could be hard, and ruthless, and quite determined when she wanted her own way."

"And—forgive me—did you give her her own way about the divorce?"

"I ... don't quite know how to answer that."

"She brought suit, didn't she?"

"Yes, we'd been living our own lives for quite a while by then. And when I say that, I don't mean what it usually means. It would have been easier, in a way, if there'd been another woman."

"I believe these things are sometimes arranged," said Antony cautiously. Douglas's laugh had an angry sound.

"I meant, if there had been, I'd have wanted the divorce. As it was—"

"As it was?" Antony prompted, after a moment:

"Oh, well, there was Clare, you know. I'd have kept things going, if I could, because of her."

"You defended the action."

"Yes." He was deep in his thoughts for a moment, living again a bleak moment in the past. "I knew I'd lose Clare if I didn't. And I lost her anyway."

Antony waited, and let the silence lengthen; but after a while he asked, quietly, "Why did Laura want the divorce?"

"She wanted a free hand with Clare. She said I interfered," said Douglas bitterly. "Looking back I can see now, after we were married, she was always possessive. But I was very much in love, you know. Then when Clare was born . . . Laura was much more mother than wife after that."

"And still possessive?"

"More than ever. And, after all . . . what defenses does a child have?"

"Very few, I suppose." And what sort of self-torment, he wondered, had produced that pathetic scrap of paper which his uncle had received? "So the divorce went through."

"It did. It's surprising how much I learned about myself," said Douglas, moodily. "Up till then, I always thought 'cruelty' meant beating your wife. But I suppose you know all about that."

Antony, rightly taking this as a compliment to his professional ability, rather than as a reflection on his behavior as a husband, said vaguely, "It's a complicated subject." And added, after a brief pause, "You'd have thought she must be desperate to be free, to put up with all the publicity." Douglas frowned at him, as though there was something obscure about what he was saying. "A sensitive woman—"

"Sensitive? Laura wasn't sensitive at all . . . she was extremely thick-skinned."

"That isn't exactly the general opinion of her," said Antony, cautiously, and with truth.

"No." It seemed he wasn't going to add anything; but before Maitland had considered where next to shift his ground the door opened, and after a moment Emmie Canning came in with a tray. He thought she looked anxiously at her husband, but by the time she had set down her burden and dispensed some rather anemic coffee she was smiling again and apparently untroubled. Antony reviewed his questions and decided that the worst was over; the remainder could be put in her presence without undue impropriety.

"How long was it since you saw Laura ... how long before she died?"

"About a fortnight; a little over a fortnight, it was the weekend she came down with flu. I took Clare for a walk, and then we got a bus and had tea in Wimbledon. When we got back I saw Laura wasn't well, and I tried to persuade her to let Clare come home with me."

"She wouldn't, of course," said Emmie, calmly. "She said I was a bad influence."

"Yes ... well." Douglas looked at her with some anxiety, but she showed no sign of concern. "What I did was telephone Barbara. She promised to look after things."

"I see." Antony sipped his coffee and wondered how much there was left in the pot. If he drank off this rather insipid mixture at a gulp, would he be likely to get a refill? "That sounds as if you trusted her," he said.

"Yes. Yes, of course," But Canning looked startled; now, what was there in that carefully worded comment to upset him?

Emmie said, disdaining circumlocution, "If you mean, do we think she killed Laura ... no, we don't."

"Thank you, Mrs. Canning." His gratitude sounded genuine. "Will you also tell me what you think happened."

"I don't know. I don't understand it," said Emmie. "But things do happen sometimes ... things you can't explain." She spoke in a rush, but her husband took his time about answering.

"There seem to be arguments against suicide. But I don't see what else it could have been."

"Did you ever think she was the type to kill herself?"

"She threatened to once or twice. I thought it was just a tale ... to get her own way," said Douglas. "Someone who meant it wouldn't talk about it. That's what I thought."

"I don't think you can generalize like that." Was Canning's new tension just because his wife had rejoined them, or was there some deeper cause? "Do you know Stanley Prior?" Antony went on, in the casual tone that was so deceptive to those who didn't know him.

Emmie said, "No," and Douglas said, "I've met him," and sounded grim as he spoke.

"He was Barbara's boyfriend," Emmie put in, quickly. And

again Antony was puzzled by something odd in their reaction to a rather simple question.

"Barbara says he wanted to marry Laura," he told them.

"Yes, I know." (Now, how could he have known that?) "She told me the day . . . the day she was arrested," Douglas went on, just as though the question had actually been asked aloud.

"Do you think —?"

"No, I don't! A chap like that!" He broke off abruptly, as though taken aback by his own vehemence.

Antony smiled at him. "Like what?" he asked, encouragingly.

"I . . . don't know really. It was just an impression I got . . . hearsay . . . nothing to go on." Canning was floundering badly now.

"You didn't think, perhaps, he'd make a good stepfather?"

He was expecting a further reaction to that, but it was Emmie who answered him, saying in her calm way. "We wanted Clare with us; we always did. You couldn't expect Douglas to like the idea—"

"No, of course." Try it another way, then. "Prior's one of the Crown's witnesses. What sort of an impression do you think he'll make?"

"He's smooth." Perhaps profiting from his wife's example, Douglas seemed to have recovered from his agitation. "He'll make a good impression," he added, grudgingly.

"I see. Well, that's a pity," said Antony, cheerfully. He was anxious now to smooth the other man down. "Can you think of anyone with a motive? Anything at all?"

"I've given that some thought, of course," said Douglas. "I wish I could help."

"That seems to bring us back to Barbara Wentworth," said Antony, regretfully.

This time there was no doubt at all about Canning's reaction. He said, "No!" violently, and threw out his hand in a gesture that sent his half-filled coffee cup flying. "What are you chaps doing?" he asked. "What does she have lawyers for if they don't do anything?"

"We can but try." Antony, to tell the truth, was rather startled by this whirlwind he seemed to be reaping.

Perhaps the mildness of his tone had its effect, for Douglas said with much less hostility, "Of course . . . I'm sorry. But we know her, you see."

Antony thought of the deserted flat in Roehampton, and Derek's strained admission, in the near dark of the kitchen, "I care most damnably what happens." He didn't want to think of that . . . he wanted to think of this as just any other case . . . do your best, and forget it. He wondered if, even without his friend's interest, he could have maintained his own detachment, and decided that perhaps he couldn't. But it was queer that he should have realized so vividly, in the desolate atmosphere of Laura Canning's home, that he believed her sister's story . . . as far as it went. Believed at least that she was innocent of murder.

Emmie had produced a cloth from somewhere and was on her knees mopping up the coffee her husband had spilled and collecting the pieces of the broken cup. The silence had been only momentary, but it seemed to make her uneasy. "It's true, Mr. Maitland," she said. "If you knew Barbara—"

"It isn't what *we* believe that matters." He got up as he spoke, and, "We can but try," he said again. "I was wondering—" he hesitated "—whether it might be possible for me to see Clare."

This time Douglas did not reply, but the hand that was resting on the arm of his chair clenched slowly. Emmie's head was bent, so that he couldn't see her expression (but surely every drop of moisture must have been taken up by now). After a moment she dropped the cloth in the hearth and scrambled to her feet. "It's so late," she said. "She'll be asleep."

"Yes, of course. Another time—"

He was watching Canning as he spoke and wasn't surprised when he said, harshly, "It won't be possible." He exchanged a glance with Emmie and then added, as though goaded by Maitland's silence, "She's been ill. She couldn't answer questions."

"That might not be necessary." Antony looked from one of them to the other. "But I'm sorry to hear . . . what's the trouble?"

"She's been under a great strain," said Emmie. She spoke flatly, almost without interest; but suddenly he realized that she was almost as tense as her husband. "The doctor said we mustn't do anything to remind her—"

"Of course not." He wondered if his hearty tone sounded as insincere as he felt.

"She couldn't tell you anything, you know," said Douglas. "She was asleep."

"In any case, I've troubled you enough for one evening," said Antony. He began to move indecisively toward the door. Emmie followed him, but Douglas stayed where he was, near the fire.

"Good night," he said, as the visitor turned in the doorway, and the finality of his tone seemed to ignore the implication that there might be a further meeting. He didn't seem to have anything to add, so Antony went out and shut the door behind him.

In the narrow hall, he looked down at Emmie Canning ad smiled, and started to say something conventional. They were interrupted by a voice calling: "Emmie. *Emmie!*" and at the urgency of the repetition she turned without ceremony and ran quickly up the stairs. Clare stood on the half landing. She was a fair child, and her fine, straight hair was cut in a style that might have been a deliberate imitation of Emmie's own. But there the resemblance ended. She was thin, and her eyes looked too large for her face; perhaps it was only the cold that gave her that pinched look? Certainly she seemed chilled, in spite of being huddled in a long, blue nightgown that contrived at once to be attractive and old-fashioned.

"What is it?" she said. "I heard you talking." There was a fretfulness about the words that made them almost an accusation.

"Just a man to see Daddy on business." Emmie stood two steps below, and looked up at her stepdaughter with cheerful reassurance. "Nothing to do with *us*," she added. "So go back to bed again and get warm."

"I can't sleep." She made no move to comply with this request. "I was . . . thinking," she said.

"What about, you silly girl." Emmie made a friendly, shooing movement. "I'll bring you some hot milk," she promised.

"I don't want . . . it is today, isn't it, Emmie?" Her voice rose as she asked the question. "I know it's today," she persisted. "Or why didn't Daddy bring a paper home?"

"He forgot, that's all. I don't suppose there was any news, anyway."

"How can you say that? How can you? When Auntie Barbara—"

"There isn't any news about Auntie Barbara. Really, Clare. We'll tell you when there is." Emmie's cheerfulness was wearing a little thin; she surged up the last two steps now and began to urge the child across the landing. "Back to bed with you; there's a good girl. What will daddy say if I let you catch cold?"

"It doesn't matter. Nothing matters." Antony couldn't see them now. The note of hysteria had gone, but Clare's tone had a flat hopelessness that was almost more disturbing. He stood looking up the stairs until Emmie rejoined him.

"You see?" she said, going past him to the front door. "It's just the shock. That stupid woman, Mrs. Paley, just rushed to tell her and made no attempt at all to break it gently."

"It must be very difficult for you."

"I wouldn't mind." Her hand on the knob, she was turning it this way and that but making no attempt to pull the door open. "She's such a dear child. I could make up to her for everything . . . I know I could . . . if only—"

"If only . . . what?"

"I wouldn't mind," she repeated, "if I thought she was getting better." Still not looking at him, she twisted the handle with sudden determination, and opened the door.

"But, surely—" Antony stood his ground, and she raised her eyes at last to meet his. He saw now that she was very near to tears.

"Nothing seems to be doing her any good. Douglas thinks . . . there are places where they understand these things." She paused, and added, desolately, "We want what's best for her, Mr. Maitland."

He wondered afterward what he had said when taking his leave of her; in face of her distress there wasn't much that could be said without downright unkindness. But going out into a night that seemed colder than ever and making his way back to the station, there were other things he wondered about, too.

8

HE HAD FORGOTTEN all about Sir Nicholas's guests and was quite taken aback when he started to cross the square and saw lights in the long windows of the drawing room. As he reached the bottom of the steps he was formulating excuses for not rejoining the revels; but perhaps if he let himself in quietly he wouldn't need to use them.

Afterward he found it a little difficult to recall exactly the sequence of events; he knew what must have happened by reasoning rather than by memory. One thing he was sure of, he had noticed no movement in the square, had no premonition of danger. And that, no doubt, was stupid after the episode of the night before.

The front door opened before he had got his key out. He took it for granted Gibbs must have heard him coming, and had stepped forward so that he was silhouetted against the brighter light from the hall before he realized that one of his uncle's guests was on the point of leaving. He stepped aside quickly then, leaving the bulky figure of Bruce Halloran, Q.C., in sole possession of the doorway; and as he did so there was the sound of a shot and—simultaneously, it seemed—the long mirror that hung at the back of the hall cracked and splintered with a noise as shattering as that of the rifle itself.

Halloran said afterward, with no very great originality, that the bullet parted his hair; and if it wasn't quite as bad as that, it was certainly a near thing. For a moment a kind of paralysis held him, more astonishment than fear; then he moved quickly, grabbing Antony unceremoniously by the arm and pulling him across the threshold.

"No, look here, Halloran, I might be able—"

The heavy door closed with a bang. Halloran said over his shoulder to Gibbs, who was hovering in the background looking scandalized, "You'd better phone for the police." But his eyes remained fixed on Antony's face, and he did not immediately relax his grip on his arm.

"Certainly, sir." The old butler wouldn't have demeaned himself by a display of curiosity, but one thing he had to know. "What shall I tell them?" he asked helplessly.

"Say we're in a state of siege," said Antony, flippantly; he met Halloran's accusing look with the flicker of a smile. "I suppose you realize," he said, "that if you were two inches taller—"

"I realize that, all right." Halloran was so swarthy that it was impossible to say he paled, but certainly he looked thoughtful. "Who gave you that black eye?" he demanded. "And just what are you up to, Maitland?"

If Antony felt there was something unfair about the unanimity with which his friends asked him this question, he didn't say so. Probably he realized what the answer would be. "Nothing at all," he protested. "I'm quite at a loss . . . oh, lord!"

All this had not been accomplished in silence. Three ladies had appeared at the top of the staircase, dressed for the street; a group of men emerged rather hurriedly from the cloakroom; and Sir Nicholas had opened the drawing-room door and was surveying the scene with a blank expression. In the background Gibbs's voice could be heard clearly: "Number five Kempenfeldt Square, Officer; I must ask you to treat this as an emergency." Antony threw a despairing look at Halloran.

"I ought to telephone Sykes," he said.

"Go ahead, then." Halloran nodded encouragingly. As Antony went down the hall toward the study he heard him saying genially, "Nothing to be alarmed about. But perhaps the ladies should wait a little—"

"You saved my life," said Antony later when the rest of the guests had gone and he was in the study with Sir Nicholas, and Halloran, and Sykes. "Hysterics just then . . . I'd never have lived it down."

Halloran, who was one of Sir Nicholas Harding's closest friends, thought that possibly the disturbance might take some living down anyway. He raised his glass with an ironical grin. "To your continued survival," he said.

Inspector Sykes, who had arrived unruffled when the local men had finished their investigations, accepted the cigarette Sir

Nicholas was offering him and said, with one of his penetrating looks, "You'll not be telling me *this* wasn't an attempt on your life, Mr. Maitland."

"No, of course not."

"And after what happened yesterday—"

"I still don't understand. And what about these racetrack toughs of yours? They wouldn't be taking potshots at me." He saw the detective open his mouth to comment, and added irritably, "I—do—not—know—of—any—reason—" He glanced at his uncle as he spoke, but Sir Nicholas was leaning back in his chair as though perfectly relaxed, and his face was in the shadow. Opposite him, Bruce Halloran nursed his glass and was obviously waiting for enlightenment.

"All the same, the two things must be tied up in some way," said Sykes. "And you did identify Badger's companion—"

"Tentatively, Inspector."

"Well, you thought it might be a man called Roberts. And Roberts is not to be found at his home, or in any of his usual hangouts."

"Is he a gunman?"

"No. The knuckles, usually. He's been known to carry a razor. The sandbag was a new departure."

"Well, you see what that means. Tonight they wanted to kill me, last night they wanted carefully to preserve my life."

"I wouldn't say that," Sykes corrected him. "My guess is, they wanted to put you out of commission for a considerable time."

"Have it your own way," said Antony, equably. "Either way, it doesn't make sense." He caught Halloran's eye as he spoke. "I ought to explain," he told him, and took the time to go into some detail.

"It couldn't be the Partington crowd," said Halloran when Antony had finished. "The only one who could have had a grudge against us was Partington himself, and he got off."

"Was that his name?" said Antony. "I'd forgotten. But you'd agree, wouldn't you, it couldn't have been our client, whatever his name was?"

"Not possibly. Not his style of thing at all," Halloran assured the detective.

"And there haven't been any—er—untoward incidents where you're concerned?" Sykes asked him. It would perhaps be unfair to say he spoke hopefully.

"Nothing at all," said Halloran; and grinned at him, his teeth very white by comparison with the darkness of his complexion.

"Not revenge," said Antony, positively. "But I'm beginning to wonder—" He paused, looking at his uncle. "Someone I could recognize," he hazarded.

"It seems to be a possibility." Sir Nicholas was unusually quiet this evening, and even now his tone was noncommittal.

"So perhaps the inspector was right when he accused me of knowing more than I was telling about the Wentworth affair."

"Now, Mr. Maitland!" Sykes protested.

"Well . . . is there anyone connected with it whom I could have seen before? There might be some sort of a racket going on at the shop—"

"I don't see what call you've got to say that," said the inspector, severely.

"—but would Madame Raymonde be able to command help from Badger and his companion?" Antony went on, ignoring the interruption.

"If I understand you," Sir Nicholas put in, "the mere mention of your name as an interested party might have alarmed someone who felt you might recognize him."

"Well, I suppose . . . there's one person, Inspector, who seems to be known to a number of the people I've talked to. But I haven't seen him yet."

This was going too fast for Sykes. He said, "Who was that, Mr. Maitland?" but his tone was reserved.

"Stanley Prior." He wasn't very interested in the suggestion himself, until he saw the detective's expression. "That rings a bell," he said, accusingly.

"No-o." But he spoke hesitantly, and looked in turn at each of his companions as he added, "I don't know anything to his discredit. And certainly nothing that would connect him with the kind of violence we're talking about."

"Good," said Antony, as though he hadn't spoken. "Tell us all about him."

"I don't know anything," said Sykes, again. "I just think he's been lucky, that's all."

"Come on, Inspector. You can't leave it there."

"Well," said Sykes, in his cautious way, "there's never been a charge against him. But when we made inquiries about him—as Mrs. Canning's fiancé, you know—there seemed to be an idea in certain quarters that he might, just possibly, have provided the inside information for some of those jewel robberies that were bothering us a while ago."

"Aha!" said Halloran, in a pleased tone. Sir Nicholas got up quietly, collected the four glasses, and went to refill them. Antony said nothing; he was well aware that the detective wasn't altogether happy about what he probably considered an indiscretion.

"Nothing positive, you understand," Sykes was saying. "Nothing more than that his name kept cropping up. And the last robbery was a year ago ... we caught the chap who did it, and he got five years. As for Prior, he has a wide circle of acquaintances and was known to be intimate with one or two of the ladies who lost their jewels."

"A year ago," said Antony, reflectively. "He might have been getting hungry by the time he decided to marry Laura Canning." In answer to which, all three of his companions spoke at once.

"This passion for making wild guesses—"

"You're going too fast for me, Mr. Maitland."

"Too impetuous by half."

Antony grinned unrepentantly. "Don't you think it might be worth taking a further look at him, Inspector?"

"From the point of view of these attacks ... I'll pass your speculations on to the proper quarter," said Sykes, dampeningly. "If you mean that we could reopen the case on the strength of them—"

"I didn't, of course. All the same—"

"No, Mr. Maitland," said Sykes, with finality.

Half an hour later, when the other two men had gone, Sir Nicholas looked at his nephew and said, "He'd have arranged some sort of cover for you, if you'd let him."

Antony's smile was a little halfhearted. "He'll do that anyway," he said. "At least, I expect they'll keep an eye on the square for a few days. I don't fancy having anyone too closely on my heels."

"All the same, you'll oblige me by taking care."

"Do you think I won't, sir? I'm not really ambitious for a star part at an inquest." He had been on his feet since seeing the visitors out and now he yawned and turned toward the door again. "What chance do you suppose I have, Uncle Nick, of persuading Jenny all this has nothing to do with me?" he asked.

Sir Nicholas looked after him. "I shouldn't even try," he advised.

THE WEATHER HAD IMPROVED next day, the sun even going so far as to put in a halfhearted appearance—though not until Antony had turned down Jenny's offer to drive him, in case there was fog later, and had already left Waterloo on the Southbourne train. Before he opened his morning paper he wondered, briefly, how they were getting on in court, and whether Derek's headache was better. He wondered, too, if he ought to have changed his plans and tried to get a look at Stanley Prior. But tomorrow, after all, was also a good day.

In court the prosecution had launched a long string of witnesses who had known the Wentworth sisters from infancy. There was a dreary sameness about their stories, and the trouble was, thought Derek Stringer, they're telling the truth, as they see it, so what's the use of trying to shake them? His head had been better when he got up, but it all started aching again halfway through the morning, probably from sheer frustration.

And some of the evidence, of course, wasn't only a matter of opinion. There could be no doubt, for instance, that Barbara, at the age of fourteen, had said "I *hate* her!" and rushed out of the house in a temper when told she couldn't go on some cherished expedition unless Laura went, too. For all Lamb's melancholy, and the matter-of-fact nature of the elderly cook-general in the witness box, it was a curiously vivid picture. And believable, thought Derek ruefully.

Nor was there any doubt that the vicar's wife was telling the truth when she said that Barbara had flatly refused to be her sister's bridesmaid. "You could tell Laura was hurt about it, and Mrs. Wentworth and I did our best to persuade her," she said. "But she was always a very determined girl, and I'm afraid she was jealous."

And so it went on. Such silly little episodes, thought Derek, savagely; the trouble was they formed a sort of logical progression, something the jury might feel they were working out for themselves. And the impact wasn't diminished by the information which recurred with depressing regularity ... Mrs. Canning had worried about her sister ... well, her job you know, a *model* ... and one didn't feel her friends could be quite, not quite the sort her family would have approved. In each case, Sir Nicholas disclaimed the desire to cross-examine with a negligent gesture, as though what had been said wasn't worth the trouble of denying. But his junior, angry and increasingly uncomfortable, knew only too well that the prosecution was making its points.

And, if he had to admit it, the prisoner's bored expression didn't help matters at all.

They saw her for a few moments just before the court reassembled after the luncheon recess, and Sir Nicholas again tried to impress on her the importance of the impression she made, especially on the jury. She listened to him patiently and then shook her head. "I think whatever I do will look wrong to somebody," she said. "If I smile they'll say I'm shameless; if I look sad they'll think it's remorse." Counsel waved a hand in reply, as though dissatisfied with her argument but unable to deny it.

It was left to Derek to say bluntly, "If only you wouldn't look quite so—so disdainful."

She burst out laughing at that, and he thought resentfully that she seemed pleased with the description. "No ... do I?" she said. "But you can't expect me to look as if I care." And though she promised before they left her to "try to amend her ways," none of them felt very satisfied with the results of the interview.

There were a few more friends of the family after lunch, and still the picture continued to emerge with overwhelming clarity: of Laura thoroughly identified with her parents, with Barbara the odd-man-out ... resentful of the position, sometimes furiously angry, and almost always indiscreet. Can't they see how it was? Derek raged to himself. He was conscious of the hostile feeling in the courtroom as an almost tangible thing. She'd changed now, or at least schooled herself to indifference. But they'd only mistrust her the more for that.

The last witness that day, and probably also the most damaging, was the solicitor from Southbourne who had looked after Arthur Wentworth's affairs. He was a tall man, and dignified, with shining gray curls surrounding what looked like a tonsure. He took the oath with a ponderous air and gave his evidence in resonant tones.

He described the family and its affairs, so far as he had observed them while his client was alive. He gave details of the late Arthur Wentworth's estate, which was a sizable one; and told how the two daughters had come down to Southbourne for the funeral after their father's sudden death. And how he had informed them of the provisions of the will ... "One hundred pounds to his younger daughter; everything else went to Mrs. Laura Canning."

"Did it occur to you that there was anything inequitable in the arrangement?" That was Lamb, underlining the point. As though it wasn't obvious enough already.

"He told me he made the decision after very serious thought." The ponderous tone had its own effect of emphasis. "I ventured to suggest that, even if the main provisions stood, a slightly more generous bequest to Miss Barbara Wentworth might be made, but I found him adamant."

"Did he give you his reasons?"

"In a way. Laura, he said, had remained at home until her marriage and had always been guided by his wishes and those of his wife. He felt that Barbara had cut herself off from the family when she left home."

"And it was your task to tell these two young ladies how things were left?"

"It was."

"How did they receive the news?"

"Mrs. Canning behaved very properly and modestly. She was much upset by her father's death and seemed touched by his thought for her."

"And Miss Wentworth?"

"She looked very white and angry. And then she asked how soon she could have the money."

"You continued to act as Mrs. Canning's solicitor?"

"I did."

"And can therefore tell us of her testamentary dispositions?"

"Indeed I can. It was a very simple arrangement—"

Perhaps Sir Gerald had been caught before by solicitors disserting upon "simple arrangements." In any event—to everyone's relief—he did not allow the witness very much latitude. "We are concerned to know whether Miss Wentworth was remembered in her sister's will."

"To the extent of five thousand pounds."

"That is, in Mrs. Canning's last will, which was made three years ago?"

"Yes. But the legacy to Miss Wentworth was also included in the previous disposition of her estate, that is, in the will made after Arthur Wentworth's death but before her divorce."

"Thank you. That is very clear." And indeed it was, thought Derek, gloomily . . . only too clear.

This time Sir Nicholas did not waive the chance to cross-examine; he came to his feet slowly and stood looking at the witness for a while before saying, "When you spoke to Arthur Wentworth about his will, did he give you any other reason that you have told us for his attitude toward his younger daughter?"

"He did not."

"No hint of irregular behavior?"

"No."

"Just that she had disregarded his desires in this one matter when she wished—as so many young people do—to leave home."

"I understood there was a general dissatisfaction."

"But no very serious matter to justify it? Would you say he was of a vindictive disposition?"

"I should say he liked to be obeyed."

"And this—er—testamentary disposition of Mrs. Canning's, under which Miss Wentworth was to inherit a small proportion of her sister's estate—"

"Five thousand pounds," said the witness, who obviously liked to have things accurate.

"Yes . . . I am glad you reminded me of the exact sum," said Sir Nicholas, insincerely. "Mrs. Canning asked your advice, no doubt, before deciding on this particular amount?"

"Well . . . yes."

"There seems to be some doubt in your mind. Perhaps you will explain."

"At first Mrs. Canning was reluctant to do anything that seemed to go against her father's wishes. I think it was her husband who persuaded her; then she consulted me."

"I see. And now perhaps you will tell us—"

It had to be done, of course, thought Derek; you have to go through the motions, even when you know there's nothing to gain. And through all the long afternoon he couldn't see that the prisoner, for all her protestations, had modified her scornful expression in the slightest. Perhaps it wasn't to be expected, but the fact depressed him.

THERE SEEMED TO HAVE BEEN some sort of a hitch. Antony got home about seven o'clock to find a scene of frenzied activity. Stringer, with the potato pan in one hand and a fork in the other, appeared in the kitchen doorway with a cloud of steam behind him; in the living room Jenny was pulling table mats out of the drawer in a distraught way and muttering to herself as she did so. Only Sir Nicholas had dissociated himself from the preparations, and was sitting in his usual chair. After one look at his expression Antony gave him a glass of the sherry he was trying to save for Christmas, and stoked up the fire, before going away to wash. When he returned, calm seemed to have been restored, and his uncle looked a little less austere.

All through the meal he had a feeling Jenny had something she wanted to tell him, but she'd get round to it when she was ready. Afterward, of course, there was information to exchange. Antony put his coffee cup on the mantelpiece, thought for a moment of Emmie Canning and her milky brew, and took his favorite position with his back to the fire.

"I hope you were right," he said, "when you thought they wouldn't reach Stanley Prior's evidence today."

"They didn't." The cigars were at Sir Nicholas's elbow. He selected one and began his careful preparations.

"But we had a good dose of motive for all that," said Stringer. He paused, and then, "It was deadly," he added, disconsolately.

"As bad as that?"

"As far as I'm concerned, it made me feel it was no wonder the damned woman had been killed," said Derek. "And that was before they got to the financial details. By the time Prior's got through telling the jury that both sisters were in love with him—" He broke off with a helpless gesture and looked up at Antony. "There wasn't a thing we could do," he said.

"Any special points?"

"Not really. Nothing we didn't expect."

"And I drew a blank, too, in Southbourne. Do you mean to call any witnesses, besides Barbara Wentworth?"

"I'm in two minds about that," said Sir Nicholas.

"It might be as well to have the last word with the jury," Antony agreeed. "However, for what it's worth, I found two people who couldn't stand the sight of Laura—"

"*That* won't help," said Stringer.

"No, but have you noticed that nobody likes them both?"

"Except Stanley Prior."

"Well, except Prior, if you like. These two could only be useful as a sort of counterbalance to what went on today. I mean, they've nothing of particular interest to say."

"That would be altogether too much to expect," said Sir Nicholas, apparently addressing the tip of his cigar.

"One is a chap called Walter Midland, who says Laura was 'calculating' and Barbara 'generous'; and the other is a school-mistress, and quite terrifying." He began to feel in his pocket for the envelope on which he had written the lady's name, but all that came to light was the sketch of the crocodile. "She says Barbara had serious faults of temperament, but jealousy wasn't among them. And before you comment on that, either of you, let me tell you that even a juryman who was three parts asleep couldn't miss the fact that she was extremely fond of her." He paused, and then added, conscientiously, "That Miss Dillon was fond of Barbara, I mean."

"I think you've wasted your time," his uncle told him. "But as a matter of interest, what did she think of Laura?" The cigar was drawing well now.

"She called her 'underhand.' I've been wondering, sir—"

"Has it occurred to you that we have had some extremely divergent opinions on Mrs. Canning?" Sir Nicholas was pursuing his own train of thought. Antony turned the crocodile envelope over and studied the notes he had made on the back of it with rather a blank look.

"Sensitive ... shy ... highest principles ... gentle. Oh, yes, and 'spiritual,' of all things. And a lot more besides. On the other hand, ruthless, calculating, underhand ... she sounds a pretty fair menace to me."

"You will not help matters, Antony, by allowing your prejudice to blind you."

"Well, sir ... what do you think?"

"Oh, I agree with you." His uncle smiled at him blandly. "But the comment remains a fair one." Derek laughed and put down the cigarette on which he had been drawing nervously, and began to drink his coffee. Jenny looked up at her husband.

"What were you wondering?" she asked.

"What sort of a hold Laura had over Madame Raymonde."

"Are you seriously suggesting—?"

"I was thinking about it in the train, and I'm beginning to feel she wouldn't have been above a little genteel blackmail."

"You're implying that Mrs. O'Toole might not have found it possible to refuse her a partnership?" said Sir Nicholas.

"And that cash might not have been the only consideration that passed. Precisely, sir."

"Where does that take us?" wondered his uncle.

"Nowhere, at the moment," Antony admitted.

Derek had heard about last night's events from his leader over the luncheon table. He said now, frowning, "You seem to be contradicting yourself. If you think madame tipped off Stanley Prior—"

"I think she's by far the most likely person to have done so, *if* he's the man responsible for the attacks. I agree," he added discontentedly, "nothing makes sense."

"Wait a minute. I have a message for you from Sykes," said Sir Nicholas. "He phoned just before I left chambers."

"Well, sir?"

"He said you might be interested to know that Prior is a frequent visitor at the house of a Mrs. Edgecombe-Daly. She's a wealthy widow and lives in Kensington."

"I don't see—"

"She is also a regular customer of Madame Raymonde's," said Sir Nicholas. "And while you're considering that, let's accept your guesswork for a moment and see where it takes us. If you recognize Prior tomorrow—"

"Well, it would depend who I recognized him as, wouldn't it?"

"Yes, I suppose ... it's infernally tricky," said Sir Nicholas, testily. "And I don't see how it's going to help us, even if he is a crook of some kind. Unless you can prove he murdered Laura Canning, and as far as I can see he had neither motive nor opportunity."

"I'm afraid not. All the same—"

"You saw Douglas Canning last night." The discussion was proceeding rapidly in circles, and Sir Nicholas abandoned it without apology. "I should have thought your talk with him would have been worth at least a brief report."

"I made some notes in the train," said Antony, feeling in his pocket again. This time he brought out a notebook and opened it at the first page. Sir Nicholas looked at it with an affectation of surprise and produced his spectacles in a resigned way. "I think they're fairly legible," his nephew added, encouragingly.

Sir Nicholas read, and passed the book across to Stringer in silence. Antony picked up the coffeepot. Jenny leaned back in her corner of the sofa, her eyes on Derek's face.

"It would seem," said counsel at last, as his junior returned the notebook to its owner, "that there is here more obvious cause for interest."

"That's what I thought, sir, until I got home last night. And I don't mean I've lost interest in the Cannings, only that the other has to be looked into as well. I'd like to see Emmie Canning during the day—"

"It would be a shame," said Jenny, "to upset the little girl and more." Antony was not deceived for a moment by her casually aloof air.

"It's not as straightforward as all that, love."

"You think she knows something?" asked Sir Nicholas, with interest.

"I've no reason to think so. But Emmie implied that Clare was ill because of the shock of her mother's death, while I'd have said she was far more concerned with what was happening to Auntie Barbara."

Derek said irritably, "What does that prove?"

"I just think it's queer, that's all. And there's another thing—"

"Well?"

"I'm not too sure whether it was *the doctor*'s opinion of her condition I was being given."

"Say what you mean," growled Sir Nicholas.

"Emmie said—" he closed his eyes, remembering " '—there are places where they understand these things.' That means an asylum of some sort ... a mental home ... psychiatric treatment .... whatever the modern jargon is. I just don't like the position, that's all."

Derek was frowning over this. "I don't see that it helps," he said, at last.

"Not as it stands," Antony agreed. He had been watching Jenny's expression, but now he turned to Stringer. "Refresh my memory," he requested. "What is Douglas Canning's job?"

"He's with the Imperial Insurance Company," said Derek. "He manages one of their head-office departments, which sounds impressive, but the salary isn't. And while Laura was alive he was paying her twenty pounds every month toward Clare's upkeep."

"Which she didn't need."

"No, but seemed fair enough to the court, I suppose."

"I seem to remember ... wasn't there a hint somewhere of financial difficulties?"

"There was some local gossip, Bellerby said. The impression was he'd found it pretty difficult, after he remarried. Certainly they've been going carefully."

"And now?"

"Well, Laura's money has gone to Clare, you know, and Douglas is her trustee, so I don't imagine they're feeling the cold," said Stringer.

Much later, when they had gone over and over everything to their common dissatisfaction, Derek went home and Sir Nicholas retired to his own quarters. Antony closed the door behind them with a distinct feeling of relief and went back to the living room. The fire was burning low, but Jenny was sitting where he had left her gazing into it as though she were hypnotized. He sat down on the arm of one of the chairs. "Now!" he said.

She raised her eyes, and he saw that she looked troubled. "I went to court today," she said. "I wanted to see her."

"Because of Derek?"

"In a way. Yes, I suppose that's really as near as I can get to the reason. They weren't exaggerating a bit about how that evidence sounded, Antony. It was horrible."

"Uncle Nick never exaggerates." This was not altogether an accurate statement. "But how did it strike you, love? If you were on the jury—"

"Well, I've heard all sorts of things they haven't, so I can't really tell. I think they might quite easily feel a lot of sympathy for Laura—after all, she's dead. Or they might feel Barbara had a hard deal all round from her family. In either case, they'd put her down as jealous, even insanely jealous ... and anything could follow from that."

"I was afraid that was how it would be. That Paley woman was 'speaking no evil' for all she was worth ... *de mortuis*, you know ... but I'd be willing to bet she hated Laura's guts. But what did you think?" he persisted.

Her eyes had turned back to the fire again, and she did not look at him as she replied, "I like her. I want to think she's innocent. And whatever she did I'm desperately, desperately sorry for her."

"You haven't mentioned the financial motive."

"Well, you see, I thought . . . if she committed murder, it wouldn't be for money."

"It's a funny thing, you know, that she never married. It can't have been for lack of opportunity."

She raised her head then and smiled at him. "That's the one thing that's obvious," she protested.

"Not to me."

"She's so beautiful," said Jenny. "But she wouldn't want to be loved just for that. Don't you see?"

"Perhaps." He sounded doubtful.

"Antony, what are you going to do?"

"Ask some more questions . . . and make some more ennemies, only too likely," he told her, with a rueful look.

"You said—I'm trying not to worry you, darling—you said you didn't know who it was that shot at you."

"I don't."

"But this man Prior—"

"It's the wildest of guesses." He got up restlessly and took his favorite place with his back to the fire, but he did not look at her as he spoke. "I just think it might be as well to know a little more about him."

"Nothing happened today . . . did it?" she asked, with sudden suspicion.

"No, I . . . don't worry so. The square's as good as out of bounds to any would-be assassins for the moment."

"I suppose—" But whatever she had been going to say, she thought better of it. "Uncle Nick's worried, Antony. I can tell."

He laughed suddenly, and sat down beside her on the sofa. "The worst thing about all this—really, love!—is that it confuses the issue."

"You mean, you've got an idea?"

"I always have ideas." He did not seem to find the thought consoling. "They're not always right."

"No, but—"

"If only there was more time, but with the trial half over . . . and it isn't enough to prove it to the jury, I've got to convince Derek, too." He got up and held out a hand to her. "Come to bed, Jenny. Who lives may learn. But I've got a nasty feeling that, whatever the lesson is, we're not going to like it."

9

WEDNESDAY MORNING saw Antony in court again, a decorous and silent satellite in learned counsel's orbit. And again the prosecution was calling on friends of the deceased woman—witnesses to Sir Gerald's thoroughness, as well as to the prisoner's malice. As he listened, Antony saw what his uncle and Derek and Jenny had meant about yesterday's evidence. If the substance was impressive, its repetition was deadly.

Barbara Wentworth this morning had an almost deathly pallor. He wondered, as he looked at her, what had made him so certain of her innocence that afternoon in Laura's flat; now he was as suddenly assailed by doubt. Had it been just sympathy . . . wishful thinking, as Derek had said? He wasn't attracted by what he had learned of Laura's character, and that might be prejudice, too. And he was desperately anxious on Derek's behalf; they had been friends too long to allow him the luxury of indifference to the other man's feelings. But it was dangerous—wasn't it?—to go into an investigation with any bias at all.

It was nearly eleven o'clock when Stanley Prior's name was called, and Antony's interest quickened, and then died again as he watched the new witness cross the court, enter the box, and take the book in his right hand when adjured to do so by the clerk. Just for a moment he thought Prior looked familiar . . . in a minute he'd remember . . . but then he thought the resemblance was only to someone he'd seen on the films. Prior was a big man who moved quickly and confidently, and undeniably good-looking. He was clean-shaven, with dark hair and eyes, a straight nose, and a firm mouth and chin. When he took the oath, his voice was pleasant; he seemed perfectly at ease, and it wasn't difficult to see why Jill found him charming. In fact, thought Antony, a ruddy paragon. The reflection did not endear the witness to him. But the worst thing was that, in spite of that elusive familiarity, he couldn't remember ever having seen the man before.

He leaned forward to break this to his uncle. The attacks were now more of a mystery than ever ... he realized, suddenly, that he had thought Prior responsible; that he had tied them in, quite definitely, in his own mind, with his inquiries concerning Laura Canning's death. Now he told himself this had been ridiculous, and wasn't much comforted even by Sir Nicholas's placid acknowledgment of the information; but in spite of everything he still watched the witness with sharp attention.

His full name was Stanley Stephen Prior, he lived at an address in Bayswater, was thirty-six years old, of independent means. Derek looked round with raised eyebrows at this last piece of information, but if Prior's source of income was as shady as the police thought it, how else could he describe himself?

Lamb was wasting no time over the preliminaries. "Now, I must ask you, Mr. Prior, whether you are acquainted with the prisoner."

"I have known Miss Wentworth for nearly three years." A courtesy that might have been expected, so why, Antony wondered, should he feel so certain that it was insincere? More prejudice? But there was something else puzzling him.

"A close friendship, shall we say?"

"We saw a good deal of each other."

"And did you also know the late Mrs. Laura Canning?"

"I did."

"How did you come to meet her?"

"Through Miss Wentworth. That was about nine months ago."

"And your friendship ripened?" (Sir Nicholas was growling to himself, but most likely he only objected to the phrasing of the question.)

"We came to know each other well." To be fair, you couldn't blame the chap for being careful about his answers; not a nice situation to be in, however you looked at it. He had a habit of touching his upper lip, which might have been deliberately adopted to give himself a little time for thought.

"Now, to turn to the day Mrs. Canning died. The eighteenth of September. Did you see Miss Wentworth that day?"

"Yes. I called for her with my car at about eight o'clock—"

"About eight o'clock, Mr. Prior?"

"Well, that's what we arranged. I don't think I was late."

"This was at Mrs. Canning's residence in Roehampton?"

"Yes."

"Did you go in to see Mrs. Canning?"

"No. My business that night was with Barbara—with Miss Wentworth."

"Please tell us where you went, and what passed between you."

"We went to Richmond, to the Unicorn. It was quiet, and we could talk." He hadn't looked once at the prisoner so far, but now his glance flickered toward her for a second. "There was something I had to tell her."

Barbara was sitting as though she had been turned to stone. Her eyes ... serene, untroubled ... were fixed on the wall above and to the left of the judge. What Medusa head had she seen there to bring her to this frozen immobility? But then her lips twitched, nervously, and she moistened them with her tongue; and Maitland thought only, the spell is broken; but Derek Stringer, watching her, felt her fear and bewilderment as though they were his own.

"I must ask you to tell us—" Lamb was saying.

"It was ... a personal matter."

Mr. Justice Carruthers coughed, a courteous intimation that he wished to intervene. "I understand you to say a matter of business, Mr. Prior."

"I used the term loosely, my lord." But it seemed, after all, that he wasn't above being rattled. "I meant ... I meant that what I had to say concerned Miss Wentworth. Well, it concerned Laura, too; I mean, it was *about* Laura. I mean—"

The judge smiled at him benignly. "Just take your time, Mr. Prior. I am sure you are going to explain it all to us quite clearly," he said.

"I wanted to tell Miss Wentworth I was going to marry her sister," said the witness, baldly.

Sir Gerald looked sadly at the judge, as if the interruption—though almost intolerable—was no more than he expected. Carruthers nodded at him. "Please go on, Sir Gerald," he invited. "I just wanted to get that clear."

"If your lordship pleases," said Lamb, in heartbroken tones. But though he might deplore the intervention, he didn't seem to have lost anything by it. "Why did you wish to give this information to the prisoner?" he asked.

"Because I ... because we had been good friends. I thought it was only fair," said Prior earnestly. And suddenly there was that quick, darting look at the prisoner again, the gesture of rubbing his upper lip, which might or might not be a nervous one. But . . . he's enjoying this, thought Antony incredulously. And something stirred in his mind, an awareness . . . only the word was too strong . . . .

"You imparted your news," said Lamb, heavily. "How did it affect your companion?"

Sir Nicholas came leisurely to his feet. "My honorable and learned friend," he said, "is perhaps in too frequent attendance in that place to which his constituents have called him. He may have forgotten that there are certain rules regarding the proper examination of a witness."

"M'lud!" exclaimed the Solicitor-General, looking as though he was about to burst into tears.

"Your question could well be rephrased, Sir Gerald," said the judge, solemnly.

"How did she look? What did she say?" said Lamb, despairingly, to the witness.

"She looked . . . very taken aback," said Prior, carefully. "And she said . . . she said—"

"Come now, can't you remember?"

"She said, 'Damn you, Stanley, you can't do that!' " His tone was apologetic. Somewhere at the back of the court a woman laughed and then was silent again.

"Was that all she said?" Lamb asked.

"Well, I suppose . . . I don't remember exactly." Just the right note of hesitation; by now Antony felt he could almost have predicted just where the pauses would come. And how did it look to the jury . . . an honest man in a difficult predicament? "Of course, she was upset," said Prior, with devastating effect. "I knew that couldn't be helped." And now the prisoner turned her head and looked at him; his eyes met hers with a sort of grave sympathy. Derek Stringer made an involuntary movement, knocking his pencil off the table with an incredible clatter. He made a grab for it, but it rolled out of reach across the floor of the court.

They didn't leave the matter there, of course; when Sir Gerald Lamb decided to underline a point, he underlined it. Question and answer were rephrased and emphasized, over and over again. Barbara Wentworth had again her guarded look, and she did not turn her eyes to the witness a second time.   But at last, "You have told us you called for the prisoner at eight o'clock on the evening of the eighteenth of September. At what time did you return to Roehampton?"

"At ten o'clock."

"Are you sure that was the exact time?"

"Well—" The witness paused. "Not later than ten," he said.

"And again you did not go into the flat?"

"No. I'd seen Mrs. Canning, earlier in the day." He paused, as though considering some addition to this statement, but said only: "I drove straight off, after Miss Wentworth got out of the car."

"Now, there is just one more point I must raise with you, Mr. Prior. Did the accused ever speak to you of her financial affairs?"

"Not exactly. She asked me once if I knew how she could raise a thousand pounds."

"When was this?"

"About three weeks before Laura died."

"And you replied—?"

"I said, why not ask Laura? She didn't seem to like the idea, so afterward I mentioned it myself."

"To Mrs. Canning?"

"That's right. Barbara must have asked her, after all, because she knew all about it."

"Had she agreed to provide the money?"

"No. I said, why not let the poor girl have what she wanted? And she said, 'To give to that creature—never!' So I let the subject drop."

"Without clarification?"

"She obviously didn't want to talk about it."

Sir Nicholas was heard to murmer, "How admirably incurious." Counsel for the prosecution was thanking his witness. The judge consulted his watch, an old-fashioned "turnip" which he kept on the desk in front of him. "The court will adjourn until two o'clock," he announced and Antony was leaning forward, shaking his uncle's shoulder.

"Partington!" he said, excitedly. And scrambled to his feet in belated deference to the judge's departure.

Sir Nicholas scowled at him. "You told me—" he began, in an accusing tone.

"It's that trick he has of stroking his lip, only *then* he had a mustache," Antony explained, not very clearly "I only just realized—" He subsided again as the court began to clear.

"You're talking of your Liverpool client, when you were acting as Halloran's junior?"

"Not our client, the chap who got off. The one we were pretty sure was behind the whole thing."

"But if he was acquitted, what possible harm can it do him to be recognized?" asked Sir Nicholas, in bewilderment.

"None at all, unless ... oh, I don't know, Uncle Nick." The brief excitement had gone; his tone was flat and discouraged.

"He may be using another name, but it certainly wouldn't do any good to cross-examine him about that." Counsel was thinking it out as he spoke. "What do you think, Stringer?"

"He'd say he was falsely accused in the first place, and even after he was acquitted it was the only way he could get a square deal," said Derek. "And for all we know it may be true."

"Exactly. So you see, Antony—"

"But if he employed Badger and Roberts ... and if he tried to shoot me ... there must be some reason, sir."

"That danger, at least, should no longer exist, now he knows you've had the opportunity of recognizing him."

"That wasn't what I meant." Antony sounded cross, and his uncle smiled at him. "And we'll have to tell Sykes, but there isn't a thing he can do, you know," he grumbled, and sustained a long, hard look before Sir Nicholas finally nodded his agreement.

IN THE DOCK Barbara Wentworth had managed to maintain the illusion of cool detachment; in the room below the court, Antony and Derek found a raging fury, too angry at first to speak coherently, almost too angry to speak at all. "But you knew what he was going to say," said Antony; of course, she wasn't ready to be reasonable yet, but if he could divert her at all she might recover her temper the sooner.

She gave him a smoldering look. "I didn't know how it would sound," she said, bitterly. "How he could!"

"He was telling the truth as he saw it," said Antony. He grinned at her. "A cad, but a truthful one," he added.

"Just wait till I get a chance to say something," she raged. "I'll—"

"You'll not get a chance," said Derek, "until you've quite recovered." His tone was apologetic but quite firm. Barbara turned on him with an incredulous look.

"I'm not ill," she snapped.

"Not ill," he agreed. "But far too angry to be allowed anywhere near the witness box."

"But you've got to call me. Sir Nicholas said—"

"You can't give evidence while you're having a tantrum," Derek told her.

"But I'm not ... I'm just ... I've a *right* to be angry."

"Every right," said Stringer, "but you can't afford to be." As this apparently rendered her speechless, he took the opportunity of adding, "Let's sit down; there are one or two things we want to know." She sat down without a word, and he followed her example. Antony moved to the end of the long table and perched himself on the corner. He was learning something, he thought; this was a side of Derek's character that he'd never seen before. It came to him that that was Derek's weakness: quick to grasp a point, good at handling a witness ... but not so good at dealing with people on a personal level; far too ready to disclaim responsibility if an interview wasn't going right, if he wasn't getting the information he wanted. But over the wayward Miss Wentworth, at least, he was obviously willing to go to some trouble. Barbara, of course, was no more genuinely quiescent than a volcano is three minutes before it erupts, but on the surface she was calm enough.

"This story about your needing a thousand pounds," said Derek abruptly. "Is it true?"

"Of course it is." She might be calm, but she still sounded resentful.

"You must have wanted it pretty badly."

"If you want to know why, you can ask me, can't you? No need to wrap it up. Of course I hated to go to Laura."

"All right then ... why?"

"There was a friend I owed a lot to. No, I don't mean money ... gratitude." There was a bleakness in her expression now; her anger had died as quickly as it had come.

Derek looked puzzled, and when the silence had lengthened a little Antony said quietly, "The girl who looked after you when first you came to London?"

"Yes. I told you about her, didn't I?"

"I think perhaps you didn't tell me everything."

"It was so much more than I can ever explain; she gave me the first ... disinterested affection ... I think I had ever known. I wanted to help her so badly ... but I couldn't."

"What was wrong?"

"She was ill. She could have stayed in a hospital, of course, but there was her little girl. That meant having someone to look after them both." She paused, and looked from one to the other of them, as though daring them to express either sympathy or concern. "As a matter of fact, she wouldn't have needed as much as a thousand pounds," she added. "I didn't know how long it would be, the doctors wouldn't say; but she died a month ago."

"What happened to the baby?"

"She's been adopted ... Mr. Bellerby told me that. And if you want the whole story, Laura disapproved because she was too damned respectable to make allowances. Maggie ... well, she did what she thought she had to, and she was kind, and she was happy. I almost hated Laura when she said no." Again her look was challenging. "Do you understand that?" Neither of the men spoke, and suddenly she gave them her most dazzling smile. "Has it occured to you," she asked, "that Laura would have been very likely to change her will when she married Stanley?"

Derek said sharply: "Do you *want* to be acquitted, Miss Wentworth?"

"Of course I do. But not if the price is too high, Mr. Stringer. Not if the price is too high."

"What exactly do you mean by that?" He seemed to be looking at her now almost with dislike.

"That I've told you all this about Maggie." She paused and frowned, as though wondering why she had done so. "But I won't tell it again in court."

"We must explain—"

"I won't!"

"You said, 'Just wait till I get a chance to speak,'" Antony reminded her.

"That was to say what I think of Stanley."

"Well, you're not going to do that," said Derek, positively.

"I've told *you*. Have I shocked you, Mr. Maitland?"

"Never mind about us. It doesn't matter if we think you're a bad-tempered vixen," said Derek bluntly, "but I'd rather not disillusion the jury, if you don't mind." For the second time in a few minutes he seemed to have reduced his client to a state of stupefaction.

"You can say you needed the money for a friend ... a private matter," said Antony; with most people he'd have hoped that, having gone so far, the rest would follow. But in this case, he wasn't so sure.

"All right. But goodness knows what they'll think, after hearing Stanley," said Barbara gloomily. The thought, only too obviously, was making her angry again. "I can't bear to think of him getting away with it," she said.

"Perhaps he won't," said Antony. Something in his tone made Derek look at him curiously. "Tell me, Miss Wentworth, do you know of any connection between him and Madame Raymonde?"

"None at all ... well, he knew her, of course ... not well."

"Think about it," he advised her.

"There was just ... but that's silly!"

"Tell me, anyway."

"When he phoned me that day ... he rang the shop to make arrangements for the evening," she explained. "He gave me a message for madame, but I thought it was just a joke."

"Well?"

"He said, 'Tell her I'll be coming round one day, to talk about Etienne.' I gave her the message, of course, and I never thought any more about it. But they didn't know each other well, Mr. Maitland ... I'm sure they didn't."

"Laura wanted to become a sleeping partner in Raymonde's," said Antony.

"I know."

"Do you think madame was seriously considering the suggestion?"

Barbara frowned at him. She seemed too puzzled now to be angry. "She turned it down once." she said. "But I had a feeling she hadn't altogether given up the idea. I don't know why she should have wanted it, because I don't think she liked Laura."

"Let's leave it at that then." He slid off the table as he spoke, and Derek pushed his chair back and came to his feet.

"We shan't reach your evidence today, Miss Wentworth," he said. "Don't worry."

"I wish to God we could get it over with," exclaimed Barbara, with a return of her former violence.

"I'll see you before then. I expect Sir Nicholas would like to, as well. Don't worry," he repeated.

The clear green eyes were mocking now. "There's no pleasing you, is there?" she said. "Is it better to be—what was your word—disdainful? Or to let the jury see what I'm really like?"

"It's a good thing for you," said Antony to his friend as they made their way to the restaurant where Sir Nicholas awaited them, "that Bellerby wasn't present at that interview."

"Why shouldn't he have been?"

"He's a great advocate of kindness to clients," said Antony.

But Derek wasn't listening. He seemed to have become infected with some of Barbara's fury. "If I could get my hands on that chap Prior," he said furiously, "I'd—"

"Leave Prior to me." Maitland spoke more positively than was usual with him. "I'm beginning to have an idea—"

"I thought you said—"

"Relax, will you?" They were outside the restaurant now, and he paused to look at his friend. "'Defense Counsel Assaults Prosecution Witness' would *not* make a good headline," he said soberly.

"Look here, Antony, what are you going to do?" asked Derek, with sudden anxiety.

"Nothing at all. I shan't go looking for Mr. Prior, but I may send him a message," said Maitland. "Meanwhile, let's get our lunch. I've got a busy afternoon ahead of me."

"Where are you going?" They paused to locate Sir Nicholas, and then began to cross the crowded room.

"To see Emmie Canning. And then to the shop." He turned to grin at Derek over his shoulder. "And if Prior really is the last prosecution witness, you'd better think of some way to persuade Uncle Nick to spend the whole afternoon between cross-examining him and opening for the defense," he said. "Your efforts notwithstanding, we daren't let Barbara into the witness box until she's had a little more time to simmer down."

"How true," said Derek. He sounded worried again, and apprehensive. It wasn't until later, when he was already on his way to Wood Green, that it occurred to Antony to wonder whether Stringer still believed that Barbara had killed her sister. He had to admit that his own declaration of faith could have done with a bit of encouragement.

10

THE DAY WAS as unpleasant as its predecessors had been, dark and chilly, with nothing whatever to cheer up or sustain the spirits. By the time he turned into Belvedere Crescent, where the Cannings lived, Antony was walking so slowly that he had become very cold indeed; the trouble was, the thought of the interview oppressed him.

If he'd been walking faster he would almost certainly have caught up with Emmie and Clare before he reched the Crescent. As it was, he saw them near the gate as he turned the corner, and quickened his pace to come up with them before Emmie had found her key. He thought the pleasantness of her greeting was a little forced,, and her quick look at Clare told its own story of her anxiety.

They had obviously been shopping, and the parcels already, at this early date, had a festive air about them. Clare, in a warm, blue coat that reflected the color of her eyes, looked prettier at close quarters, though her face still had the pinched look he had noticed when he saw her before. She greeted him with polite docility, but when he caught her eye again a few moments later it seemed to him that, for all her apparent listlessness, she had a wary look. Emmie led the way into the house, talking nervously all the time, and the other two followed her. It was perhaps just as well, Antony thought, that in the circumstances she could hardly bar the door against him.

"We've been up to Oxford Street, to see the shops. And then we had lunch; it was fun, wasn't it, Clare?" She dumped her parcels onto the hall table, paused a moment, and then turned to face them again. "Have you got the parcel with the new crayons? You could try them out in the kitchen; it will be warm in there."

"All right." Clare did not sound enthusiastic, but she went without argument. Emmie followed her fussily.

"I'll just pull the door to, dear; then you won't be in a draft."
Over her shoulder Antony could see Clare's expression as she
turned her head to acknowledge this consideration; passive, yes,
but frighteningly aware.

In the afternoon light, the drawing room had a bleak, thread-
bare look. It was also quite fantastically cold, and he wasn't
surprised that Emmie hadn't taken her coat off. She spent longer
than was necessary lighting the fire, rather as though she thought
it would go out again immediately if she took her eye off it. But at
last she could delay no longer; she got to her feet again and turned
to face him.

"Well?" she said. It wasn't an aggressive query; in fact, there
was a quiet resignation about it that was at once pathetic and
disarming.

"I think you know why I've come, Mrs. Canning. I'm hoping
you'll let me talk to Clare."

"I can't," she said. And then, "You saw how it was the other
night."

"She seems better today."

"Yes, but ... the least thing upsets her. And this week ... we
can't let her go to school, you see. There might be talk."

"I suppose so. And she's more concerned for her aunt, isn't she,
than shocked by her mother's death?"

"No ... oh, no! How can you say that? She was devoted to
Laura." The very choice of words made the protestation mean-
ingless ... something she had read in a book.

"Naturally." If there was a dryness in his tone, she found his
smile reassuring. "What was Laura like ... as a mother?" he
asked.

"I'm afraid she was demanding." She turned to look down at the
fire, and perhaps she was disappointed to find that it did not need
her attention. "Shall we sit down, Mr. Maitland? I think it will be
warm quite soon."

"Thank you." He moved from where he had been standing to
take the chair she indicated—the one Douglas had sat in the last
time he was there. "You were saying you thought Laura was too
demanding," he prompted.

"Yes, and ... and jealous." From the tone of her voice you
might deduce that this was a very bad crime indeed in Emmie's
calendar. And suddenly she was talking almost eagerly. "I only

know what Douglas has told me, of course. He used to be so worried ... she didn't like Clare to be fond of him; she was even jealous of her affection for Barbara. I remember one day he told me she'd said to him, 'I heard them laughing together'—Clare and Barbara—and she made it sound as if it was a crime."

"The general opinion seems to be," said Antony, casually, "that Barbara was jealous of Laura."

"Don't you think, Mr. Maitland, that people are inclined to see their own faults in other people?" She was putting forward an opinion, and she did so hesitantly, as though his agreement was the last thing she expected. "I mean ... Laura thought Barbara was jealous of her, but really it was the other way round."

"It was Laura who had everything," he objected.

"She didn't think so. I know I sound spiteful," she added apologetically, "and I daresay you think I can't see her straight because ... well, because. But Douglas is a very kind person, and he says Laura always felt that Barbara had taken all the things that really mattered; she'd have liked to be independent, and not care what people thought of her, and really beautiful. I suppose," she added, thoughtfully, "one might feel rather extinguished if one had a sister like Barbara."

Antony thought of Stanley Prior, that morning in the witness box. It wasn't so straightforward, after all, what had happened between the three of them. Emmie was looking at him anxiously, and he said, on an impulse, "Mrs. Canning, have you ever asked Clare about that evening?"

"Of course I haven't. I mean ... she told us, and then she cried, and we never asked her about it again."

"Was it the doctor's idea to avoid the subject?"

"He said to take things easy and she'd be all right. So Douglas thought ... we both thought—"

"It might be the best thing for her to get it off her mind," he said.

"Is that why you want to see her, to ask her about all that?"

"Yes, of course. But I'll make you a promise, Mrs. Canning. If you'll let me talk to her, I'll do nothing to bring the subject up .. unless she mentions it first."

"I don't see how that would help you," she objected.

"Let's say I've a very optimistic nature."

"She won't talk about what happened," she warned him. "She never does."

"Still, I'd like to see her."

"I hope I'm doing the right thing." She got up as she spoke, and looked at him uncertainly. "It might do her good to talk to somebody else," she said, persuading herself. "If you really promise—"

"I really do. But don't disturb yourself, Mrs. Canning. If I might just go into the kitchen and see how she's getting on with those crayons—"

"I don't think I should let you."

"Please do." But he knew as he spoke that it wasn't his persuasions that weighed with her, it was some inner certainty of her own that prompted her to sink back into her chair again.

"Very well," she said. But as he turned to smile at her from the doorway he found her eyes fixed on him, wide and worried, and he wondered what on earth had possessed her to give her consent.

He stood a moment in the hall and closed his eyes and wondered—now that he had got what he wanted—just what he was going to do with the opportunity. Then he went to the kitchen door and opened it and went in.

Usually, once he had been in a room, he could have given a pretty fair description of its arrangement and its contents. Now he knew only that the kitchen was cmfortably warm, and that Claarle—for the moment completely absorbed in what she was doing—was sitting at the center table under the light with a yellow crayon in her hand and a thick sketching block in front of her. She did not look up immediately, but when he said, "May I come and talk to you? Emmie's busy," she raised her head and gave him the same warily comprehending look he had seen on her face before.

"Please sit down." The assumption of dignity was absurd, and touching. "Are you a friend of Emmie's?" she asked.

"A friend of a friend," he told her, cautiously. "And I came to see your father the other evening."

"That was business," she said, quickly, as though it were somehow important to be reassured on the point.

"Yes, of course. But sometimes the two things go together. For instance, I might come to you to have my portrait painted, and we might become friends, too."

"That would be fun." And suddenly he was startled to see in the child's eyes the impersonal, but at the same time almost fanatical, assessment of the born painter who is faced with a new subject. But it only lasted a moment. "I've been doing a picture to go with daddy's Christmas present," she confided. "I've bought him a pullover, so the picture's of him wearing it." He went to look over her shoulder at the sketching pad. "I don't think I'm very good with crayons yet," she said doubtfully.

Privately he thought if this wasn't very good, her best must be quite an achievement. There was the drawing-room mantelpiece, with the old-fashioned wooden clock, and the tall candlesticks at either end; and there was Douglas in a canary yellow sweater, with tension in the set of his head, and in every line of his body. It was quite alarmingly revealing that his daughter should see him in this way. At the other side of the fireplace sat Emmie, undeniably roly-poly in a long, flowered housecoat; her hands were folded in her lap, and the whole effect should have been one of repose . . . if it hadn't been for the fact that she was perched on the edge of the chair and that her eyes were fixed with painful intensity on her husband's face.

He stood looking down at the picture for some time before he moved from his position at her shoulder and pulled out one of the wooden chairs. "I like it," he said, mildly, and was glad to see that this rather tepid praise seemed to have struck the right note. "Is the dressing gown your present to Emmie?" he asked.

"Yes, of course. But I thought I'd put it in Daddy's picture," she said, tilting her head a little as though to see her handiwork in a different perspective. "I like Emmie, don't you?" she asked suddenly, and raised her eyes to meet his with a strangely anxious look, as though the answer was somehow important to her.

"Very much."

"I'm going to be an artist when I grow up, and I think I'll paint people's portraits, but Miss Cowley says it's too early yet to know what I'll want to do." She pushed the sketching block away a little and sighed for no very evident reason. "What do you do?" she asked. It was a relief, he thought with amusement, to find her social instincts so far developed; so that she was quite ready to bear her fair share of keeping the conversation going. But the question was awkward, in view of his promise to Emmie.

He hesitated and then said, "I'm a barrister," deliberately choosing the word with which he thought her less likely to be familiar.

"That's a . . . sort of lawyer, isn't it? Do you help people?" Her face had its pinched look again; she picked up a pencil from the table and held it tightly in both her hands.

"I try to."

And suddenly she was speaking with an eagerness that jumbled the words until they were almost unintelligible. "Daddy said nothing would happen to Auntie Barbara, because her lawyers wouldn't let it. Do you think that's right? He *said* it ... really he did ... but no one talks about her now." The quick, stumbling words ceased, and the look she gave him was full of hurt bewilderment. "Do you know what they say about her?" she demanded.

"Yes. I know."

"She didn't!" she told him, with a fierceness that reminded him of Barbara herself.

"I know that, too." (Was that the truth? But you couldn't speak of doubts to a child.)

"Are you ... one of hers?"

"In a way."

"Then tell me ... tell me!"

"Emmie told you the truth, Clare. There's nothing to tell you yet." He watched the eagerness fade from her expression.

"Then ... could you give her something? I don't know how to send it." She did not wait for his reply, but got up and went across to the dresser. After a moment's rummaging in one of the drawers she turned with another picture in her hand, and held it out to him in silence.

It was a watercolor portrait mounted on stiff board, larger than the sketch he had already seen and more finished. In fact, it was extraordinarily good, though he thought the faults of technique were more obvious than in the rougher drawing; it was extraordinarily good ... and it terrified him. Here was Barbara Wentworth ... the glorious hair, the proud set of her head; Barbara as she might be ten ... twenty years from now, with lines about her mouth and shadowed eyes. But here, too, was the repose he had looked for in vain in the picture of Douglas and Emmie ... more than that, a serenity. He looked up to find the child's eyes fixed on him anxiously.

"You're frowning," she said. "Don't you like it?"

He didn't seem to notice the question. He said in a shaken tone, "Is that what Auntie Barbara looks like to you?"

"It *is* what she's like," she told him, confidently. But then her mouth drooped. "I thought you'd understand," she said, with all the desolation in her tone of one who knew her vision to be unshared.

"I think I do." Now, with what eyes did Douglas see his daughter that he thought her mad? Because that was what Emmie was suggesting, wasn't it, in the hall on Monday night? And if they were sincere . . . he raised his head and looked at her directly. "Clare . . . if I asked you to help Auntie Barbara—?"

"I can't help her. There's nothing I can do." Her voice went up on the assertion.

"Perhaps I could show you the way."

"If you make a promise you have to keep it, don't you?" The question was so unexpected that it took him off balance for a moment.

"I'm not asking you to promise anything," he said, but she shook her head impatiently.

"I didn't mean that."

"Well then, we ought to keep our promises. But sometimes—"

"Always!"

There seemed to be some obscure importance about the question. He said carefully, "If things happened that the person who made you promise couldn't have foreseen . . . well, the easiest thing is to ask them." And straightaway he knew he had said the wrong thing. She sat down again at the table and put her head down on her arms and began to cry.

"Nobody understands," she wailed.

He did not try to stop her tears, but after a while he got up and put his hand on her shoulder and shook her gently. "I'm taking the picture, Clare," he said. "What shall I tell Auntie Barbara?"

She raised her head after a moment, and he went across to fetch a box of tissues from the dresser and put them down where she could reach them. "I'll give her your love," he said.

"Yes . . . please." Her voice was thickened by crying, and she kept her eyes averted. "I'll find you some brown paper," she said, "you can't carry it like that." Only when the portrait was wrapped did she look up at him; she was dry-eyed now, but he was conscious of her loneliness. "I wish you'd understood," she said.

"I'll try to," he promised. They shook hands solemnly, as though they were sealing a bargain.

11

HE TOOK A TAXI back to town and stopped in Kempenfeldt Square before going on to the shop in Knightsbridge. Jenny was out, and he wondered if she'd gone back to court again; he left the picture with Gibbs and asked him to put it in the study.

It was about four o'clock when he reached Raymonde's, and he hadn't bargained for business being in full swing. He felt vaguely, and illogically, resentful that Derek hadn't warned him of this when he mentioned his errand, but it was no use worrying about that now. The sooner he got it over, the sooner he could get home and see what Uncle Nick thought of the portrait of his client.

As he pushed open the door a rush of warm, faintly perfumed air came out to meet him. Here was an alien atmosphere indeed . . . a long way removed from the familiar battleground of the courtroom, perhaps even farther from the homely comfort of the house he had just left. Three women were sitting on spindly gold chairs at the side of the room, with madame in attendance, talking volubly. Only one of them turned to look at him (he swore to Jenny later that she used a lorgnette). As he hesitated Jill shimmered out from the archway at the back in a long gown of gold lamé; she was looking unnaturally solemn. He watched unbelievingly as she glided down the room toward the group of women, turned, smiled for a moment, walked again. But she must have seen him standing there, because when she went back through the archway Dorothy came out almost immediately, bypassed the customers, and joined him near the door. She gave him her sleepy smile, but her eyes were anxious.

"We can't tell from the papers," she said, without preamble. "How is it really going?"

"It's too early to say." He couldn't tell her, after all, "As badly as possible," though that was true, unless . . . "I want to talk to madame," he said. "May I wait until she's free?"

"You'd better come through to the back. Unless you'd rather stay here." His expression must have answered her, because she began to move down the long room ahead of him. They passed Jill in the archway—this time the dress was a brilliant emerald green—and made their way into the congested space beyond. Antony perched himself on a cane-bottomed chair, which for no apparent reason was as tall as the old type office stool; but he prepared to slide off again when he saw that Dorothy was still on her feet. "It's all right," she told him. "Madame will go mad if I sit down and crease this skirt."

"Are you busy? Am I keeping you?" He glanced back into the salon, where Jill had stopped her gyrations and stood poised in an improbable attitude while an animated discussion went on around her.

"Not unless someone else comes in. Mrs. Lassister always likes to see clothes on Jill."

Antony took another look through the archway. One woman, it was obvious, was the leader of the party; the others were present only in supporting roles. "For her daughter?" he hazarded. Dorothy shook her head. "But she can't think she'll look like *that*," he protested. "If she can get into the dresses at all, which I doubt."

"Whatever she chooses will have to be altered, of course." Dorothy seemed amused. "But the fact won't be openly mentioned, so everyone will be happy." She glanced back in her turn toward the salon; the fair girl was coming toward them now, with something like a prance in her walk ... perhaps the green dress had been sold. "And if she thinks she looks like Jill does when she wears it," said Dorothy indulgently, "will it matter very much?"

Jill came in in a swirl of taffeta. "Undo me, will you? She wants to see some afternoon things now." She turned her back on her friend and looked down at Antony. "Mr. Maitland—?" she said.

"There's no news yet," said Dorothy, quickly. "Did she buy the dress?"

"She did. And I'm glad it's going," cried Jill. Every time I put it on I keep thinking how it would have suited Barbara. Oh, well!" She whisked away from them and disappeared behind a curtain at the end of the room, but a moment later she stuck her head out again to ask, "The red dress—the one madame calls garnet—do you mind? And that rather peculiar blue one."

Their talk thereafter was interspersed with her goings and comings. When she had slunk through the archway again in the garnet "creation" (Antony was beginning to realize what Barbara had meant about acting), he asked Dorothy abruptly, "What do you remember about the day Laura Canning died ... the last day Miss Wentworth was at work here?"

She hesitated before replying, considering the question, considering whether the protest, "How can that help?" would be well received. She said, at last, "It was just a day like any other."

"For instance, did she seem herself that day, was she cheerful?"

"She was fed up with staying with Laura, I can tell you that. Why, she hadn't been out anywhere for nearly three weeks."

"She went out that evening," he pointed out.

"Yes, but she nearly said no when Stanley called her. In fact, she did say so at first; only I happened to be in here while she was talking to him and I told here not to be such an idiot, a change would do her good, and she'd said herself that Laura was better."

"So she changed her mind?"

"After we'd argued a bit, back and forth. I've been wondering, Mr. Maitland ... the papers haven't mentioned him as a witness—"

"He gave evidence this morning."

"Was he ... would what he said harm her?"

"It didn't help." He made an abrupt, dissatisfied gesture. "And here I am," he said, "running in circles round the problem and getting no nearer the center."

"I was afraid," she said, sadly, "that he might be spiteful."

"I'm not even sure if it was that. It may have been just a completely invulnerable self-conceit. Have you seen him at all since Miss Wentworth was arrested?"

"That's what I don't understand. He's been in and out quite often. To see madame," she explained.

"Would you say he had some business with her?"

"I suppose that was it. I don't think she likes him coming."

"I don't suppose she does." He was thinking aloud, an indiscretion he didn't normally permit himself, and only realized that his tone had been unduly vehement when he found her dark eyes fixed on him questioningly. "Forget it," he said. "Have you ever heard the name Etienne?"

"No, I don't remember—"

"Etienne?" said Jill, reappearing through the archway in a

close-fitting wool frock whose color reminded him of Jenny's cerise paint. "He's a friend of madame's ... or at least she knows him."

"Tell me about him. What's his other name?"

"I don't know." She had paused to be unzipped, and now her voice came out to them from behind the curtain. "But I heard Barbara tell madame one day that Stanley wanted to see her about Etienne."

"Do you remember when that *was?*"

"The *last* day," said Jill, simply.

"Did she seem pleased about it?"

"That's funny ... no, she didn't. She looked dreadful, sort of gray. But then I thought it couldn't be anything to do with the message, and Barbara didn't seem to notice; and afterward so much happened I just forgot it again." She rejoined them, demure in a charcoal-colored dress made from loosely woven material. "Sackcloth and ashes, *I* call it," she said over her shoulder. "And it's absolutely the last, Dorothy ... if she doesn't like this, I'm through!"

Ten minutes later, Antony was again following Madame Raymonde up the stairs. She was talking as she went ... she was good, that little Jill, very good; two gowns—models—and to an old skinflint like that ... but he was under no illusion that she had been pleased to see him. From the top floor came the hum of sewing machines and the chatter of high-pitched voices, and then they were in madame's own room, and she had closed the door behind them, shutting off the sound.

"Well, *m'sieur?*" she said.

"Si vous le préférez, madame, causons en français; ce sera probablement plus facile pour vous."

As he hoped, that shook her. *"Mais vous ne m'avez pas dit—"* she told him, reproachfully. He could see her trying to remember ... what had she said, that other time ... how had she given herself away?

"Vous ne me l'avez pas demandé," he said; and smiled at her.

"Ah, well. It is of no matter. We will speak in English, in French, as the fancy takes us. To me it makes no difference."

"I want you to tell me, *madame*, everything you know about Stanley Prior." It made no difference to him, either, and he had made his point.

"But what is there to tell?" She swept past him and seated

herself in the straight-backed chair she seemed to prefer. "You may sit if you wish, *m'sieur*, but I hope you have not come to waste my time."

"You could tell me, *madame*, of your own connection with him."

"My own ... you are talking nonsense—he is a friend of a girl I employed, no more."

"A friend also of Etienne?"

He saw her recoil from the name; but, of course, it wasn't going to be easy. "I believe they were acquainted," she said.

"Who is Etienne?"

"Someone I knew years ago ... oh, but casually!"

"Very well, *madame*, we will go the long way around. What sort of a hold did Laura Canning have over you?"

"This is to insult me, *m'sieur*."

"*Soit!*" He shrugged as he spoke, and found himself thinking, inconsequently, how the affectation would have annoyed Sir Nicholas. "But tell me, you said she interfered in your affairs; you also said, if I remember, '*Elle l'emportait sur moi complètement.*' What did you mean by that?"

"I am sure you are capable of so simple a translation." Her voice sounded thin ... anger, or fear, he couldn't tell.

"I think she knew something about you," he said slowly. "I think she could have used her knowledge; she didn't need money, of course, but could you have refused that partnership she wanted? And would you have liked being still under her thumb?"

"This is all guessing, *m'sieur*. If it is not deliberate lies."

"It's something the police ought to know, isn't it?" he challenged her. "It won't be difficult for them to find out—"

"No!" She was leaning forward now, gripping the arms of the chair. "They are not interested any more in Laura Canning," she said.

"I wouldn't count on that if I were you. Barbara Wentworth may be found guilty, but there's always the Court of Appeal. Some new evidence as to motive—"

"You cannot ... you are worse than she was ... worse even than that man Prior," she moaned.

"My motives are far purer." He had been standing all this time, but now he went forward and took a chair not too far from where she was sitting. "You may as well tell me," he urged. "If it doesn't help Barbara no one else need know. Can't you trust me?"

"Me, I trust no one," she declared, dramatically. "If I tell you it is because you will only make more trouble, *en dénichant bien de choses inconvenables.*"

"Well, then?"

"It is this Prior who found out about Etienne. He met him in France, three, four years ago ... *quel scélérat!* And how they come to speak of me I do not know, or how he comes to know where I am now, or what I am doing ... it is a sin, is it not, that he should interest himself in my affairs? After leaving me for so long to make my own way ... to starve, perhaps."

Antony thought she showed very little sign of starving, but prudently he didn't say so. "Etienne was your husband?" he asked.

"But this I am telling you! So he say to this Stanley, there is my wife, she has done well for herself. That was all, but for me it was too much!"

"I don't quite see—"

"But it is obvious. He thinks, perhaps there is something here for me, or perhaps not. No harm to see. So one day when he is idle he walks past the *salon* at closing time, and he see Barbara ... and I do not ask, me, how he gets to know her. And he forgets about my affairs."

"But not forever."

"*Malheureusement.* Gradually he learns a little of my history, so far as it is known to her. I do not blame her; where is the harm? She tells him of my dear Michel, whose death left me so heartbroken—"

"Were you married to both of them?"

"But yes, *m'sieur.* What would you? When I am deserted, abandoned—"

"You'd reached the point," said Antony, hastily, "where Prior had found this out."

"Yes, but he does not trouble me then. He has other fish for the frying pan," said Madame. "And when he tells that Laura about it, it is for a joke, you understand. But she ... she is worried, is it right to keep silence, is it right for her to leave her own sister in ignorance of the truth? That is how she play with me, *comme la chatte se moque de la souris*; and all the time I think she will not tell, but how can I be sure? Even when she tells me what she wants, it is all hints; perhaps, after all, it is not for her to judge, but rather to help me. And I can do very well without her help, but what can I do, *m'sieur*? She is bad, that one."

"I see. And what about Stanley Prior ... what's his racket?"

"That he likes women, I know; also that he is attractive to them. I think that he lives by his wits, *m'sieur*. But chiefly on his knowledge of women."

"And it was on those lines that he approached you ... with a request for money?"

"Not at first; I have explained all that. *Et, comme il voulait se marier, il avait besoin d'une somme d'argent assez importante.* And so he asked me ... me! And I tell him, I am in such straits, such difficulties, that hardly do I know where I shall find a meal. But all that is before we hear of Laura's death."

"Was that the first time you heard from him on the subject ... the message he sent you the day she died?"

"Yes, and he came to see me that night, after he had been with Barbara. But later, when he knows that after all he cannot marry Laura, he sings a different tune. He has no longer the need to deceive her into thinking him a wealthy man—"

"Not a quick turnover, after all, but a steady income?"

"That is so. Blood will not come from a rock, I tell him ... and I am penniless ... destitute. So he tells me we shall be partners ... I shall tell him which of my clients is wealthy and lonely. And perhaps I shall make it easy for him to meet these ladies. Partners ... *pouf!*" said madame, gesticulating more violently than ever. "For him the ... easy touch, is it not? *Et qu'y a-t-il là pour moi?*"

"From what you've told me, silence," said Antony, choosing to take her literally, to her obvious indignation. "Can I not expect so much ... from a gentleman?" she asked, spreading her hands.

"You implied he was a confidence trickster," Antony objected. "You can't have it both ways."

"*Je suppose que c'est trop espérer!* And what about you, *m'sieur*? I am at your mercy after all." In spite of himself, Antony grinned at her.

"Let's get this straight. You were married in France to Etienne?"

"In 1930. I am young, and it is a romance, I think. And five years later ... everything is over! So I come to England;" she paused, and darted a look at him, rather as though there was a question which might be put here which she would rather not have to answer. "And a year later, there is my dear Michel."

"Michael O'Toole?"

"Do I not tell you? And so . . . shall I turn my rack upon the world . . . *me faire religieuse?* One must, after all, be reasonable."

"One must, indeed. So you married him, as well?"

"But I do not regard Etienne as my husband anymore," she said earnestly. "So where is the harm? And later, I think perhaps he has been killed . . . during the occupation, you understand? But he bears a charmed life, that one."

"And in 1950 your second husband died?"

"That is true. And there is money, a little, and so I start this *salon.* And I use my own name, Raymonde; perhaps that is how Etienne started to find out, if he chanced to visit London. But that is bad luck, I think, for it is not an uncommon name."

"Did O'Toole leave a will?"

"No. There was no need. He had no family at all . . . nobody! And I am his widow, am I not?"

"Well, strictly speaking . . . no." He sounded apologetic, but she gave him another of her reproachful looks. Despite her air of injured innocence, it was obvious she understood the legal position well enough, and that this was the reason she had been prepared to submit to blackmail. "Tell me, *madame,* when Laura Canning spoke to you about Etienne, did she tell you how she knew he was still alive?"

"I ask her, of course . . . but she does not tell me."

"Prior was more open with you?"

"I thought *she* had told him. He laughed . . . that first night. But later he explained to me that it was he who had met Etienne." She looked at him shrewdly, weighing the answer he might give her. "And again I ask you, *m'sieur* . . . what are you going to do?"

He evaded the question. "This partnership of yours, has it become active?" He saw her look of inquiry, and added slowly, "And Prior? *N'avez vous pas essayé de lui présenter une nouvelle victime?*"

"Ah, no, *m'sieur.* That was a matter for thought, for—how do they say?—stalling." But the virtuous tone didn't even begin to ring true.

"Mrs. Edgecombe-Daly?" he suggested.

"But that is just to do her a favor." His lack of finesse pained her. "She is so unhappy, and now . . . a different woman!"

"Will she still be happy when her new investments prove a failure, or when her jewels disappear? Or are his intentions honorable, do you think?" If his tone stung her, she made no sign.

"What could I do, *m'sieur?* I am in his power, am I not?" Her gesture disclaimed responsibility; her dark eyes were bright and indignant. "On what do I live," she demanded, "if I lose my *salon* because there are inquiries?"

Antony got up. "You could always go back to Etienne," he suggested without sympathy. He wasn't surprised when she surged to her feet in an access of outraged dignity.

"Am I then to sell myself? But you are English . . . you have no heart!"

"None at all. But my profession, *madame,* has taught me to be discreet "

"Then you will not interfere? *Ah, m'sieur, je vous remercie de votre bonté.*"

"Did you mention it to Prior when I came to see you before?"

"But, of course!"

"And did you say I seemed to be taking an interest in him?"

"That, too. There was no reason—"

"None at all. Well, I won't interfere in your affairs; but I warn you, those inquiries you fear may be made for all that."

"Then all is lost. I am ruined . . disgraced—"

"If you will tell Prior, *madame*—" But he had to wait for her lamentations to cease. "Tell him of this interview; tell him, if you like, that I recognized him; and be sure to say that Mrs. Edgecombe-Daly was mentioned in our talk."

"But, how then will this be of benefit to me?"

"Perhaps it won't. But I assure you, *madame,* it's your safest course."

"I do not understand. But if it makes him run away . . . for me that is a good thing, and so—perhaps—I will tell him." She eyed her visitor thoughtfully. "If you are thinking that he has killed Laura, I must ask you, *m'sieur,* why should he do this? Besides, he could not have done so; he was with Barbara, was he not, that evening?"

"We might get over both those objections," said Antony. He

moved to the door and paused with his hand on the knob. "But if we're talking of Laura's death, *madame* . . . neither objection applies to you." He went out quickly, before the tide of her impassioned protest could overwhelm him; and he thought, he hoped, he'd done all he could to see that his message got through to Stanley Prior.

Downstairs, all traces of the day's activities had been tidied away; everything was quiet and orderly and only one light shone, dimly, at the back of the showroom; but as he approached the door he found that Jill was waiting for him.   "I thought I'd stay to let you out," she said. "I forgot to ask you, Mr. Maitland . . . you said you'd tell me about Clare."

"I . . . don't think there's anything to report." The question chimed with his own thoughts so completely that he sounded startled. Jill said nothing but stood looking up at him in the half-light, waiting for some amplification of what he had said. "Tell me, the times you saw her with Miss Wentworth, how did she strike you?"

He thought she frowned. "A little subdued, but gay enough when she got going," she said carefully.

"Not at all abnormal?"

"Only in being a little quieter than most kids are nowadays. Mr. Maitland—"

"That's what I thought, too," he assured her.

"You're worried," she said, almost as if it were an accusation. But when he did not reply she made no attempt to question him further.

They left the shop together in silence.

WHEN HE PAID OFF his cab in Kempenfeldt Square he saw there was a light upstairs, which meant that Jenny was home again. Later he'd have to talk to Uncle Nick; but now perhaps, for a little while, he could relax and try to get his thoughts in order. But things weren't going to work out quite like that.

In the big living room everything should have been as usual. Jenny was curled up in her favorite corner of the sofa, and she turned quickly to greet him but her eyes had a troubled look. Derek Stringer came to his feet as the door opened, with as much force as if a spring had been released.

"Well?" said Antony. And then, "What's up?"

"There was another witness," said Derek. His agitation showed in both his looks and voice. "They called him after we'd finished the Prior."

Antony closed the door carefully and came a little way into the room. "Someone the prosecution sprung on you? That isn't like Lamb."

"Well, it was fair enough, I suppose." Stringer's grudging tone seemed to belie what he was saying. "The chap only turned up this morning; he's been in the States for nearly two months."

"Well?" said Antony again.

"He's a neighbor of Laura's. He saw Barbara came home the night Laura died. He's sure it was the eighteenth, because it was the day before he went away. He says she was talking outside for nearly a quarter of an hour to a man who'd just left the flat."

"But—"

"He was taking the dog for a walk," said Derek. "As he went out he saw a car draw up, drop her, and drive on immediately. Then a man came out of the house—you remember the two doors? Well, he's quite sure it was from Laura's side. They obviously knew each other, and stood on the pavement talking. When he came back from his walk they were still there, but before he came up to them the man walked away, and Barbara went into the house."

"After all, we knew she wasn't telling us all the truth." If he meant the words to be consoling, they were singularly ineffective.

Derek said, violently, "But, don't you see . . . after what Prior said this morning, what *can* the jury think? They'll think this is the 'creature' Laura talked about, that Barbara wanted money for . . . they'll think she's protecting him . . . they'll think it was a conspiracy." His voice dropped, but oddly the effect was to give an even greater emphasis to what came after. "They've gone home to think about that," he said. "Carruthers adjourned early. And honestly, Antony, I don't see how they can fail to think she's guilty . . . do you?"

12

SIR NICHOLAS WAS already in the study when Antony went down after dinner, but there was an extra coffee cup on the tray, so his visit was not unexpected. When he walked in, Sir Nicholas was standing by the desk, carefully removing the wrappings from Clare's portrait of Barbara Wentworth. He looked up and smiled.

"I take it this was left here for my attention," he remarked. "I've been wondering—" The last piece of brown paper came off, and he held the picture at arm's length. "Well, now," he added, after a pause.

"What do you make of it?" said Antony. He had come down with only one thing in mind, to talk about the new witness. But now he remembered how eager he had been earlier in the day to know his uncle's reaction to the painting. Sir Nicholas propped it up on one of the chairs and backed away to get a better view.

"Is this a new hobby?" he inquired. "If you feel you need something to occupy your leisure hours—"

"At the rate things are going, I'm more likely to take to the bottle."

"I trust not . . . so crude," murmured Sir Nicholas, refusing to be diverted. "Now this painting . . . you say it isn't yours?"

"Not mine. Clare Canning's."

"Is it indeed? It isn't perfect, of course—"

"The artist is only eleven."

"Precisely. It's a remarkable piece of work. Is the child as perceptive as this would seem to indicate?"

"I think so. I mean, I think she knows things about people without knowing she knows them," said Antony, obscurely.

"Try again, from the beginning," his uncle advised him, kindly.

"I think she knew—consciously or unconsciously—that Barbara hadn't always been happy, and that was the only way she could show it . . . by making her look older."

"And the serene look? Which, if I may say so, seems entirely uncalled for," he went on thoughtfully.

"I suppose . . . I suppose she felt Barbara had lived up to her beliefs, been true to herself." Antony paused, contemplating this statement, and added bitterly, "Why do I always manage to sound such a fool when I try to explain anything serious?" Sir Nicholas smiled gently but made no reply; and Antony, who had come downstairs quite prepared for squalls, began to feel definitely uneasy. There wasn't much to be done when Uncle Nick got angry, short of calling out the riot squad; but at least you knew where you were. "Derek told me the prosecution had another witness," he said, pushing the remark out in a tentative way as though doubtful of its reception, as indeed he was.

"They had." He did not attempt to amplify the statement, but when Antony started to speak he interrupted impatiently. "Before we discuss that you'd better tell me the results — if any — of your afternoon's activities." He gave the portrait one last, searching look, and went to sit in his usual chair by the fire.

" 'If any' just about describes it," said Antony, gloomily. He poured two cups of coffee, placed one at his uncle's elbow and the other on the mantelpiece, and took up his own favorite position on the hearth rug. "I saw Emmie Canning, and she let me talk to Clare—"

"I had gathered as much," said Sir Nicholas, sipping his coffee.

"Yes, sir. But she obviously had misgivings about it, and when she tells her husband I'll probably be about as popular as a nettle in a nudist camp."

"Much as I admire your gift of imagery," his uncle told him coldly, "I trust you will remember that there are times when it should be kept within bounds. In court, for instance." He broke off, because it was quite obvious that Antony wasn't listening.

"I'd better tell you," he said. And sat down as though he were suddenly very tired, leaving his cup of coffee marooned out of reach on the mantelpiece.

He paused hopefully when he had finished the account of his visit to Wood Green, but Sir Nicholas made no comment, merely passing over his empty coffee cup and waiting in silence for a refill. "And then, I suppose, you went to the shop," he prompted.

"Yes. I saw the two girls first," Antony told him. He paused and frowned. "I say, Uncle Nick, why do you suppose Jill put a thing like a muslin bag over her head every time she changed her dress?

It couldn't have been to keep her hair tidy . . . I mean, it didn't."

"I am always pleased to hear how you have been amusing yourself, but is the question really relevant?" Sir Nicholas wondered.

"Not really. I was just talking to them while madame was with a customer—"

"Lipstick!" said Sir Nicholas suddenly, as thought a revelation had been vouchsafed him. Antony gave him a blank look. "To keep her lipstick off the models she was wearing," his uncle explained, adding unkindly, "I should have thought any fool would have known that." Antony went back to his narrative, and the older man listened without change of expression until he came to the end.

"That gives Mrs. O'Toole a motive, of course. But Prior could have had no reason to wish Laura Canning dead."

"There might be one we don't know about."

"Possibly. But he had no opportunity. He's the one person who couldn't possibly have been in the flat that night."

"He's a chap who uses delegates," said Antony, stubbornly.

"In a matter like that . . . a case of murder?" He did not wait for a reply, but went on to another question. "We've decided, however—haven't we?—that he arranged the attack on Stringer, and probably shot at you himself on Monday night."

"I think it's obvious, don't you?"

"The motive, at least, is far from apparent."

"Well, I can remember a lot more *about* Partington than I could about his appearance, if you see what I mean. He was a clever chap, and the number of chances he took during that trial in Liverpool was quite fantastic. He admitted blandly that he'd known the other defendants, that he'd been associated with them in various business deals, that he'd placed bets at their instigation. In all innocence, of course. And the jury believed him."

Sir Nicholas smiled at his disgusted tone. "That doesn't explain what's been happening the last few days," he pointed out.

"No, but I've got to give you the picture. The others were all busy trying to blame each other for what happened; he didn't play it that way, he still couldn't believe his good friends were guilty of anything dishonest. You know the kind of thing."

"Very well."

"I don't wonder he disappeared after it was over. For one thing, the local police knew well enough what he'd been up to, and once his nice little swindle was made public it wouldn't have been possible to operate it again. So he had to change his business, but the trickery persisted; it was something inherent in his nature. And it was equally according to his nature that he should turn to women as a source of income. Am I making sense, Uncle Nick?"

"Your guesses, so far, are not too outrageous," Sir Nicholas admitted.

"All right, then. Sykes may be right about what he was doing up to a year ago; inside information is absolutely vital to a jewel thief, and would be well paid for. But his partner in this enterprise was caught, and perhaps he had no ambition to take over the active side of the business himself. He must put his abilities to a different use, and now it was no longer enough to know whether a woman had jewels or not; she must also be lonely, and preferably without anyone to advise her. I think we can assume he was hard up when he proposed to Laura Canning; and we know he was desperate enough after her death to blackmail Raymonde into finding new victims for him. I asked her about Mrs. Edgecombe-Daly, by the way; she admits having made the introduction."

Sir Nicholas was staring down into the fire. "Enter Demon King," he remarked, without looking up.

"Exactly. I don't suppose he liked getting mixed up with the police again when Laura died, but he said his piece like a good boy—even with some enthusiasm—and it seemed the matter would end when he had given his evidence. Then he went to see madame one day, and she told him someone called Maitland had been to see her. I expect he wanted to know if I'd asked any questions about him; and I can just hear her saying, maliciously, 'But yes, of course, my dear Stanley.' And he wondered where he'd heard the name before."

"I should think he remembered perfectly well," Sir Nicholas corrected him. "You say yourself that Halloran was after *his* blood. He'd remember the pair of you and read your cases with particular interest when they appeared in the press. Your own activities have not been unattended by publicity, you know."

"I know, sir." He was too occupied with his speculations to bother much about the sting in the tail of that last remark. "Say he remembered, then. He may or may not have realilzed you couldn't use the information about his checkered past; he certainly knew if I saw him and remembered him I'd be likely to ferret out his present racket and put a stop to it. And he's a man who takes naturally to violence; that was abundantly clear from our client's evidence in Liverpool . . . he'd been terrorized into compliance with the scheme. Do you think, by the way, I should ask Halloran for the details? I'm a bit vague about it now."

"I can't see that it would do any good at all, and it might prove a temptation next time you're short of cash," said Sir Nicholas. "But to return to your reconstruction, Prior, although he has given up racing, still has connections with the racing fraternity . . . on the shady side of the picture. Your friends—"

"Badger and Roberts."

"Yes. They were to put you out of action for a while. You might even have lost interest in the Wentworth affair by the time you were about again; at least, he would have had a chance to wind up his present plan. But you reacted rather violently. Roberts probably balked at making another attempt—"

"—and Prior decided the safest thing was to take a gun and do the job himself. I say, sir, it's a good thing Halloran isn't quite as tall as I am."

"It might have saved me the price of a new mirror," said Sir Nicholas, callously. "The insurance people will no doubt feel I am to blame if my guests are shot at when leaving the house. Gibbs, however," he added, more cheerfully, "is quite convinced the fault is yours."

"Like so many other things." Antony's tone was one of gentle resignation. "Anyway, that's Prior's motive for the attacks . . . don't you think?"

"I am more concerned to know . . . what next?"

"Did you speak to Sykes?"

"I phoned him from chambers before I came home."

"I don't suppose he was wildly excited by the information," said Antony, grinning.

"Not exactly. He seemed to assume it was just a preliminary to some further disclosure." Sir Nicholas was not amused. "I tried to convince him that was the sum of our knowledge . . . I hope I was telling the truth."

"At least, if madame delivers my message, that should take care of the Edgecombe-Daly woman." It was not lost on Sir Nicholas that his nephew ignored the question implicit in his last remark. "And, as you pointed out yourself, Prior can't have any further reason to be after my blood ... which you may or may not think a cause for rejoicing."

"Hm," said Sir Nicholas, declining to commit himself.

"All the same, I wish we could have caught him out, given the police something definite on him."

"Nothing he does is really our concern unless it affects Barbara Wentworth in some way."

"No, but I don't like these chaps who live off other people's weaknesses. And I don't know how it is—perhaps because she's such an unrepentant old sinner—I'd like to see madame off the hook."

"If your message results in Prior deciding to operate in a different area, that will, of course, have the desired effect. But while you may condone Mrs. O'Toole's inheriting money which would have been almost certainly intended for her, even if her 'husband' had known the truth, you can't possibly allow her to become an accessory—"

"She understands that, Uncle Nick. And, as you say, if Prior takes off—"

"A prospect I view with equanimity," said Sir Nicholas, "having had a somewhat lengthy exchange of views with him this afternoon."

Antony grinned again; he couldn't help it. "How long did you keep him, sir?"

"For over an hour and a half ... following the urgent representations of my learned junior."

"He was quite right. You couldn't let Barbara Wentworth into the witness box until she'd cooled down."

"When you consider," said Sir Nicholas, ignoring the interruption, "that there was just one question which I could usefully ask him, you will perhaps enter to some degree into my emotions."

"One question?" Antony sounded vague; he hadn't been giving much attention to the tactical details of the defense.

"Miss Wentworth is going to say that he implied he hadn't yet asked Mrs. Canning to marry him. The discrepancy is not really of any great importance, but I should like to have shaken him on this small point at least."

"You preferred to reconcile their statements?" Neither of them was conscious of the suggestion of parody in the wording of the question.

"Certainly I did. You might even say I succeeded." There was a definite bitterness in Sir Nicholas's tone. "I asked him whether he was sure he didn't say to Miss Wentworth that he was going to ask Mrs. Canning to marry him? And he said he might well have put it that way ... to be tactful you know. He said it was all arranged and wasn't a secret in any way; but he'd asked Laura not to tell her sister, to let him do it."

If he hadn't been so worried, there would have been some humor to be found in Uncle Nick's outraged expression. Even as it was, "I'd like to have seen Carruthers's face by the time you'd finished," he remarked.

"He bore it very well, though Lamb was a trifle restive," Sir Nicholas admitted. "But I expect they both knew well enough what I was about."

"Lamb had it all ways," said Antony, mournfully. "Even a nice down-to-earth financial motive, in case the jury don't fancy the psychology he's been dishing out. I suppose there was no shaking Prior about that, sir ... about the one thousand pounds she wanted, I mean."

"We touched on the subject, of course. But I didn't seriously try to make him go back on his story, since I gather our client is perfectly ready to corroborate it as soon as she is given the chance."

"At the same time calling dear Stanley all the names she can lay tongue to. Which brings us, sir—doesn't it?—to this new witness Lamb's dug up." He knew his uncle hated to be hurried, but surely by now he'd had enough leeway. "What does Barbara have to say about the man she was talking to?"

Sir Nicholas tightened his lips. "She insists that there was nobody," he said bleakly. "The witness must have been mistaken ... it was someone else he saw. And that after I'd spent the best part of half an hour trying to shake the identification."

"Could he describe the man?"

"Very inadequately. He thought he was slightly built, and a little shorter than his companion."

"Oh, dear!" As a comment it might be inadequate, but Sir Nicholas saw his nephew's frown of concentration, and for once had no retort to make. "That settles it," said Antony, after a moment. He got up as he spoke, an abrupt, jerky movement, and began to prowl about the room.

"You seem to have reached some conclusion," said Sir Nicholas, still unnaturally mild.

"We'll have to call them ... Douglas Canning and Clare." He halted for a moment and stood looking down at his uncle, but not as if he saw him.

"You think she knows what happened?"

It may have been the note of shocked incredulity in Sir Nicholas's voice that brought Antony out of his fit of abstraction and sent him striding down the room again. "Of course she knows!" he said, over his shoulder.

"But ... but—" Perhaps he did not know himself how the sentence should have ended; in any event, the protest was stillborn. His eyes followed his companion, past the desk to the window and back again. And, just for the moment, their roles were reversed, the younger man dominant, with no trace of his normal, casual air; the elder watching him with a passivity that was just as uncharacteristic.

"Don't you see, Uncle Nick, we've got to! We've got no choice!" And in spite of his insistence there was an appeal in the words that could only be born of uncertainty. Don't let the decision be mine alone ... if I'm wrong ....

Sir Nicholas stretched out a hand for his cup and picked it up and drank. He did all this slowly, deliberately ignoring the tension that was building up in the quiet room. "Stringer tells me," he remarked, "that you've succeeded in persuading yourself of Barbara Wentworth's innocence."

And was even that true? Was he right, or was it all illusion? "That's not exactly how I should have put it," said Antony dryly.

"Are you sure you know what you're doing?"

"I know ... God help me!" He had stopped his pacing now and was looking down, staring at his uncle with an odd blend of anxiety and bewilderment.

"There have been cases," Sir Nicholas reminded him, "where the calling of children by the defense has been anything but advantageous."

"Spare me the precedents ... I'm only too well aware of it."

"Then I must trust your judgment." He saw Antony's expression change and added quickly, "I'm not denying responsibility. If we call them, it will be my decision."

"Thank you, sir." He shivered suddenly and turned to look

accusingly at the fire, athough the room was warm. The temptation to let things drift, to let the trial run on to its inevitable conclusion, was almost overwhelming. Even when the verdict was in, could he be sure it was wrong? "We've no choice, have we?" he said, and was glad to hear that his voice was steady. He turned from watching the flames and smiled at his uncle.

"I'd better phone Bellerby." Sir Nicholas got up but did not immediately make for the telephone on the desk. "You'd better have some whisky," he said, in a matter-of-fact tone. "Jenny will never forgive me if you've caught a cold."

"Thank you," said Antony again. He took the glass that was held out to him and drank as if he were thirsty. Sir Nicholas raised his eyebrows but did not otherwise comment, and made his leisurely way across the room to the desk.

"It occurs to me," he said, "that I should prefer not to take this matter up with our client until after she has given her evidence."

"You think she'll object?"

"Object? Of course she will." He paused, with his hand on the phone. "I'll get Bellerby onto it right away," he said. "And then you must tell me, Antony, just what you want me to persuade that poor child to help me prove."

13

THE NEXT MORNING Sir Nicholas opened the case for the defense, briefly and in an oddly noncommittal way. From where Antony was sitting he could watch the play of expression on Derek Stringer's face, and he wondered, uncomfortably, whether his friend's anxiety was as obvious to other people as it was to him. Probably not, though anyone who was familiar with his usual impassive look might be forgiven for speculating about the change. And from there his mind jumped inevitably to the question, If the verdict went against them, how would Derek take it? He'd a nasty feeling this obsession went deep, and in spite of his depression he smiled to himself when he remembered Jenny's comparison with "the man in the song."

Mr. Justice Carruthers saw the smile and thought that perhaps, in spite of the absence of fireworks so far, Maitland might have something to surprise them with. As he saw it now . . . a sad case, thought the judge, but nothing out of the way; he wasn't even sure where the blame lay for what had happened. But that witness last night . . . trust Lamb to produce him, like a magician performing his most spectacular trick, with no sign of pleasure, nothing but a profound melancholy; that witness certainly had altered the whole look of the case . . . introduced a hint of the sordid, an unpleasant suspicion of intrigue. And even before that it had seemed the prosecution had everything they wanted ... they could prove opportunity, the evident dislike between the two sisters, and the later rivalry about that good-looking, untrustworthy fellow, Prior, who had given evidence the day before. And when I say "untrustworthy," do I mean I won't accept what he said? the judge asked himself, and decided that, perhaps, that would be going too far.

Sir Nicholas was speaking with less than his usual single-minded concentration. One hint of his intentions and he would have on his hands a completely intractable witness, capable of any indiscretion. Bellerby had questioned his decision not to tell her . . . they couldn't proceed without her consent, and was it quite right to delay like this? But that point wasn't bothering him. His present quandary was simply, how much could he safely say? Too much for the prisoner, his client . . . too little for the jury; or was it possible to strike a happy mean?

Stringer thought he was making a pretty good job of it . . . under the circumstances. He had heard without apparent emotion the decision to call the two extra witnesses, though he foresaw difficulties ahead when they told Barbara what was proposed. She'd been almost violent . . . no, delete the "almost" . . . at the mere suggestion, once, that Clare's evidence might be helpful. Now, with the end so near, had they a better hope of persuading her? For himself, he doubted it.

Barbara Wentworth had again her guarded look. This was the worst day, wasn't it, when she must break her silence and speak in her own defense? Derek was no longer angry with the stubbornness that kept her remote, disdainful, that forbade her to compromise in the least way in telling what seemed to her the truth. He had come, painfully, to a sort of understanding of the reality behind that cold façade, of the pride that would not let her show her hurt. But there was one thing she'd been lying about . . . he'd known that all along, and now he knew what it was and it wasn't much consolation. The man she had been talking to outside her sister's flat that night . . . the man she was protecting . . . .

Could you believe anything she said, after that? Could you believe she wasn't lying when she swore she was innocent? However much you wanted to trust her . . . however much you felt, looking at her, that here (if anywhere in the world) you could find integrity, and an honesty too transparent to fear the truth.

In the witness box she continued to seem remote from the proceedings, though she had a smile for Sir Nicholas when she turned to face him, almost as though she were welcoming an old friend who was visiting her. There would be no difficulty, of course, about the examination-in-chief, though there might well be some embarrassment; they knew already exactly what she would admit, what she would deny. But he dreaded the cross-examination; there were questions Lamb would ask that he felt it was intolerable she should have to answer. Perhaps she was

cleverer than he thought, but it wouldn't help her in the end ...
there was only this mad idea of Antony's ... he'd followed him
before, of course, through schemes as wild as this ... but now it
was so vitally important, and Antony seemed so unsure of himself.

But when the court rose, Barbara was still answering Sir
Nicholas's careful questions.

Antony went home and had lunch with Jenny. He wasn't going
back to court that afternoon, and he felt he couldn't bear to watch
Derek's attempts to pretend everything was normal and then give
himself away over and over again.

Jenny hadn't been back to the court since the first time. "You've
talked about her so much I feel I know her," she said, absentmind-
edly slicing more ham than they needed. "So it would seem like
spying ... especially today." They were in the kitchen—Antony
was beginning to have quite an affection for the gaily colored
chairs and curtains—and the formality of the trial seemed to him
momentarily to be very far away. But then Jenny put down the
carving knife and gave him a worried look. "That new witness
Derek was talking about," she said.

"What about him, love?"

"I said before, whatever she did I wouldn't blame her. But if it
was for some man—"

"It wasn't! That's the only thing I am sure about, Jenny ... it
wasn't that."

"Does Derek know?"

"I gave him the benefit of my valuable opinion." He smiled up at
her wryly. "I don't think he believed me, though."

They talked of other things after that, but it wasn't really a very
cheerful meal.

OF ALL THE THOUSANDS of square feet in the magnificent new
building which houses Imperial Insurance, the company had seen
fit to allot to Douglas Canning a miserably small proportion, a
narrow slip of a room screened off from the end of a much larger
one. Throughout their talk that afternoon they spoke in low tones,
oppressed by the inadequacy of the partition, though later it
occurred to Antony that this care had been unnecessary. Not the
most determined eavesdropper could have heard what they were
saying above the racket of typewriters and accounting machines
in the room beyond.

Canning received him unsmiling. "I'm glad you've come, Maitland. I was going to get in touch with some of you people tonight."

Antony took the chair that was being indicated. He wasn't quite sure how he was going to handle this, though he'd been worrying about it off and on since the night before. "The subpoena has been served, then?" he said, cautiously. The question was waved aside.

"That doesn't matter. But Clare! You've seen her once already. What do you want from her?"

"Exactly what we want from you, Mr. Canning. The truth."

"Oh, my God!" Was this the final blasphemy, a prayer uttered without hope? Douglas clenched his hands on the desk in front of him, but there was no hiding the fact that they were shaking. "She's ill," he said. "You can't—" But even the protest was made despairingly.

"I'll admit you can delay matters on medical grounds. But the court won't leave it there, you know. Unless you're sure *any* doctor will agree she's unfit to testify—"

"Of course I'm not sure. How can I be?"

"Your own doctor—?"

"We've had her to a psychiatrist. He said she was deeply disturbed . . . well, I could have told him that," said Douglas, angrily. "But I know . . . I tell you, I know . . . she isn't fit." He paused, and evidently the words he sought were hard to find. "She's only a child," he said at last, inadequately.

"I'm sorry." If there was genuine regret in his tone, to the other man it was overlaid by an unmistakable relentlessness. "Haven't you read the papers?" Antony went on.

"Yes." His voice had been low before; now it was no more than a whisper.

"Then you know we can't leave things as they are. Whatever happened that night, we've got to have the truth."

"You think . . . as things stand . . . she'll be convicted?"

"I've thought so all along; now I'm sure of it." He spoke more roughly, perhaps, than he had intended, and knew a moment's regret when he saw Douglas recoil from the blunt statement.

"And Clare can help you?" There was no resistance now, and very little bitterness. "But . . . this way?"

"It's too late," said Antony. "It's all we can do, now." He paused, and added more gently, "Everyone will be very kind to her, you know."

"Kind!" said Douglas. He turned his head away and seemed to

be staring at the brightly colored calendar on the wall ... a snow scene ... somewhere in the Alps, perhaps? After a long time he said, wearily, "I'm not proud of what I've done. But all I wanted was what was best for her."

Antony got up and, after hesitating for an awkward moment, went away without another word.

DOWN IN THE STREET again he paused, unable to make up his mind. He didn't want to go back to the court ... to the long agony of Barbara's cross-examination; Lamb, for all his sorrowful air, could be quite a deadly opponent, and today he had all the weapons he needed, conveniently to hand. How would Barbara take it ... quietly, or with the furious anger that seemed only too easily roused? But he didn't want to go back, even to find that out ... he didn't want to, and it wouldn't help anything. It was up to Uncle Nick now ... and Clare Canning. And that set off another, even more uncomfortable train of thought. Had they any right to ask a child ... ?

It was bitterly cold, and the fog which had lifted for the last day or two was creeping back from the river. He turned up his coat collar and decided as he did so that he'd go back to chambers. It would be warm, and he needn't talk to anybody; just for the moment his mind was almost completely blank. He did not move

The fog was perceptibly thicker when he reached the Temple, and followed him relentlessly into the building where Sir Nicholas had his chambers, and up the stairs to the door. Willett, emerging from the clerks' office, gave him a knowledgeable look and went ahead to make up the fire. When he had done so he picked up the overcoat which Antony had discarded untidily, said, "You'd like some tea, Mr. Maitland," without bothering to make the words a question, and went away without further attempt at conversation. Antony went to his usual chair and sat there, leaning forward and holding his hands to the fire. For the moment his mind was almost completely blank. He did not move until the clerk came back, five minutes later, with the tea.

It occurred to him then that if Willett was walking round him on tiptoe and refraining from his usual chatter, he must be in a pretty bad way. He roused himself to say "Thank you," and added, as the clerk turned away, "What do you think of the statement that the end justifies the means?"

Willett paused in mid-flight. He was a young man who never walked if it was feasible to run, and rarely stopped talking unless there was good reason to do so. "Actually, I don't think much of it," he said, cautiously, because whatever Mr. Maitland had in mind, it obviously wasn't all that simple.

Antony picked up his teacup and held it between his hands as though they were still cold. "You're right, of course," he said, uncertainly. "The question is, what will the harvest be?" He found Willett's eyes fixed on his anxiously. "Never mind. If I were a philosopher I could doubtless find some comfort in the situation. As it is, let's say it's damnable and leave it at that."

"Just as you like, Mr. Maitland." He started toward the door again, thought better of it, and turned. "I shouldn't worry," he advised. "If I was in trouble there's no one I'd rather trust . . . no one." This time he made the door and went out closing it behind him; Antony was left wondering why all barristers' clerks were omniscient (or gave every appearance of being so), and what he himself had done to deserve this unexpected tribute. He drank his tea gratefully, and didn't notice that he was burning his tongue.

Nearly an hour later, when the shadows were already deepening in the big room and he hadn't bothered even to turn on the desk lamp, the phone rang and he roused himself to answer it. "We're just leaving, Mr. Maitland," said Hill's voice, with its usual note of apology. "Is there anything you want?"

"If it's as late as that, I'm going home, too," said Antony, coming rather abruptly out of his reverie. "But go ahead, I'll make sure the door's locked."

Everything was quiet when he went out a few minuts later, but when he opened the outer door the landing beyond was dark. He began to fumble for the switch, leaving the door open with the hall light streaming out; and he was still thinking of nothing in particular, except that Hill might have had more sense than to turn out the light on the staircase.

"Don't bother," said a voice just behind him. "You won't be needing the light out here." As he swung round he saw that two men had come out of the shadows at the foot of the second flight of stairs: a burly man, whose face seemed for the moment only vaguely familiar, and Stanley Prior. The light from the hall glinted on the dull steel of the revolver in Prior's hand.

Antony had been preoccupied, but now the shock ripped

through his somber mood, leaving him alert again, and wary. "You startled me," he said, and added, with truth, "I wasn't expecting—"

"But you recognized me, when you saw me in court?"

"That's why," said Antony, vaguely. "I thought you'd realize—" He let the sentence trail, and Prior laughed; but there was no amusement in his eyes.

"I don't think you quite grasp the situation, Mr. Maitland," he said. "But our business could be better completed inside than here on the landing." He gestured with the revolver as he spoke, and Antony went back a pace or two but stopped in the doorway.

"You ought to be careful with that thing, it might go off." He was watching Prior as he spoke, and didn't like what he saw. There was a viciousness about the man that had never been allowed to manifest itself either time he saw him in court.

"Stranger things have happened," Prior agreed. "Why do you think we're here?"

"I was never fond of guessing games."

The burly man growled, "Cut it out!" His voice was gruff, and there was something about the belligerence of his tone that sounded oddly in Maitland's ears. But he hadn't time to think it out. Prior said, "Get inside!" and took a step forward, and Antony, seeing his expression, decided the time had come to obey and backed through the open door. Prior followed him, and the big man came after, pausing to close it firmly before coming up to his companion's side again. Seeing him now in the full glare of the light, "Of course, we've met before," said Antony, cordially. "On Sunday, in Kempenfeldt Square." (What was the chap's name ... Roberts? The one who'd hit Derek, anyway. But that didn't explain what he was doing here.)

"Told you he'd recognize me," said Roberts, without gratification. "You did ought to have made a job of it before this."

Prior ignored the reproach. He looked at Antony and said coldly, "I've been talking to Raymonde. I don't like interference, Mr. Maitland."

"My message was really more in the nature of a warning, you know."

"You thought I'd run?"

"It would seem advisable, don't you think?"

Prior laughed. "I am going abroad," he admitted. "But I don't like unfinished business; we've a score to settle first."

The implications of this were not lost on Antony, but it was no use wasting time in cursing himself for a fool. Prior might want his death, or he might have in mind something less drastic; probably the latter, or why had he brought a companion? But however it was, Roberts was definitely the weaker member of the partnership; if he could be disposed of somehow . . . .

"You realize, of course," he said, "that we may be interrupted."

"If you mean Sir bloody Nicholas," said Prior, "he's gone to talk to Barbara. And we watched the clerks leave. I think we've time enough." Antony began to edge backward toward the door of Sir Nicholas's room, an evidence of agitation which Prior observed with pleasure.

Roberts did not seem to share this confidence. He looked significantly at the weapon in his principal's hand. "Better get on with it," he advised.

"Don't be a fool! Why do you think I brought you along?" The burly man had definitely a downcast look. "You might have thought better of that lark," he suggested. Rightly or wrongly, Antony thought he sounded nervous.

"Well, I haven't," said Prior, shortly. His eyes were uncomfortably intent. "But first I want—"

"If you want to talk," said Antony, "we may as well be comfortable." He was very near the door of his uncle's room now, and he turned quickly as he spoke, and pushed it open, and went through into the darkness. The abruptness of the movement seemed to take his visitors by surprise. He crossed the room to the fireplace, heard Prior stumble against a chair and exclaim profanely, and then Roberts found the light switch.

"Here!" he said. "What do you think you're doing?"

Antony was on his knees on the hearthrug. "Mending the fire," he said, without looking round. "It's a cold night, isn't it?" If he'd read Prior's character and intentions wrongly, this might well be the end; if he was content merely to kill . . . .

"Leave it," said Prior, forcefully. "Damn it, do as I say!"

"We may as well be comfortable," said Antony again. He went on raking the ashes with the heavy poker. A heaven-sent opportunity, surely, for the nervous Mr. Roberts to take him unawares. There was a pause, and then he heard a cautious footstep behind him, then another. If he could judge his time now . . . .

He waited until he could hear breathing close behind him, and took a backhanded swipe with the poker. There was a howl of pain as it cut across Roberts's shins; at the same moment Antony straightened up, catching the burly man with his left shoulder as he did so. He hadn't really hoped to wind him, just to take him off balance; but for the moment, at least, the luck was with him. As Roberts doubled up in agony Antony let go of the poker and dropped the big man in his tracks with the same vicious blow he'd used in the square four days ago. At the time he had a queer sense of unreality, as though the scene were being played in slow motion; it was only later he realized that all this had taken place at lightning speed. Roberts went down without another sound, and Antony straightened and looked across at Prior, who had perched himself on a corner of the desk with an air of unconcern.

"Admirable, Mr. Maitland. Quite admirable. But you won't find this quite so easy to deal with." The slightest movement of the revolver emphasized Prior's meaning. "I admit you had me fooled; I didn't think you had the nerve—"

"You forget," said Antony. "I watched you give your evidence yesterday."

"I don't see—"

"You were enjoying it, weren't you? You were making Barbara pay for something, though I'm not quite sure what she'd done to you. If you mean to kill me you'd like me to see it coming. A shot in the back would be too kind . . . no fun for you."

"Much too kind! As a matter of fact, I may be forced to shoot you, but I shall regret the necessity."

"Will you, though?"

"You mustn't credit me with any squeamishness. And you're quite right, I did enjoy putting Barbara in her place. I blame myself, of course," he added, with an air of frankness that made Antony long to hit him. "If I'd been more tactful with her she'd never have done it and I'd be married to Laura today."

"Do you really think that . . . that Barbara killed her?"

"Don't you? All this troublemaking, and it hasn't really got you anywhere, has it? Even now . . . it's annoying, this delay, but I'll probably have less trouble with Roberts when he comes round than I'd otherwise have done."

This didn't seem to make sense. "Trouble? With . . . him?"

"He doesn't really hold with murder," said Prior, rather in the tone of one who apologizes for the amiable foible of one of his friends. He saw Antony's puzzled look and added, with a laugh, "I should have explained . . . he's going to strangle you."

There didn't seem to be much to be said in reply to that, and it took him a moment to be sure his voice was steady. Then the sheer illogicality of the situation overcame him. "But he has no reason," he protested.

"I told you there were things you didn't know. You recognized him, didn't you, as one of your assailants on Sunday night?"

"Yes, but—" In spite of the cold fear that was creeping into his mind, he couldn't help thinking of the sort of questions he'd have asked himself about that in court. He'd recognized the photograph in the Rogues' Gallery, a little doubtfully, as the man he'd seen; and now he recognized Roberts as the man in the photograph. "But *why?*" he asked, incredulously.

"If you mean, why did he attack you in the first place . . . I persuaded him," said Prior. "As for his present motive, he has a number of convictions—I forget how many—for crimes of violence. The last time the judge warned him he'd be likely to get a term of preventive detention if he appeared again on a similar charge." He paused, and his smile widened. "Are you beginning to get the idea? If you live, you can put him away for a long time, and he doesn't like the idea. Whereas if he strangles you—noncapital murder, Mr. Maitland—he won't be much worse off, even if he is caught; and he may well get away with it altogether."

"But all this, I gather, was not his own idea."

"Fortunately I was able to show him where his real advantage lay." It was ridiculous, of course, but something in the way he spoke roused in Antony's mind an unwilling sympathy for the unconscious man.

"And until he comes round," he said, reflectively, "you don't want to shoot me."

"I want you dead." There was no doubt now about the viciousness of his tone. "I'll shoot if I have to."

"You won't get away with it. The police—"

"They've nothing on me."

"They hadn't . . . until you tried to kill me."

"There's no proof of that."

"Probably not. But their suspicions will be enough to make them wonder about you if I'm found dead."

"No harm in that." There was something horribly chilling in

Prior's confident tone . . . as if he needed any further discouragement.

"Even a charge as accessory—" But he wasn't going to get out of this by talking, and there wasn't much chance now that anyone would come back to chambers. Not on a night like this, with the fog thickening . . . much better to get straight home.

"I told you, I shan't be around," said Prior. "You've made it impossible—haven't you?—for me to stay in England. And as I've come into money—"

"Mrs. Edgecombe-Daly?" (Now why hadn't he considered the possibility that Prior's schemes with regard to the lady might already be complete?)

"Yes. She was extremely interested in certain investment possibilities, and quite understood the need for secrecy; in fairness to my godfather, you know, who gave me the tip."

"The one who's 'something in the city'?"

"That's right. And you know I saw Raymonde."

"I assumed as much from the fact that my message reached you."

"Didn't you also guess, she's afraid of me. And when I had talked to her, she was still more afraid. You shouldn't have promised to keep your mouth shut, you know."

"Shouldn't I?" The tone made the words no more than a courteous inquiry; but from where he stood he could see the doorknob begin to turn slowly . . . slowly . . . soundlessly. With an effort he fixed his attention on Prior. "I'm afraid I haven't your experience in these matters," he said.

"She contributed to my expenses," said Prior. "Not a large sum, but there will be more to come from that source, when I need it."

"I suppose you'd do a good deal for money," said Antony, scornfully, his eyes on Prior's face.

"A good deal; but I wouldn't trust you, Mr. Maitland."

"Do you think I'd try to bargain with you?" The door was opening now. "You've been used to easy game for too long. You may have had some courage once, when you were operating in Liverpool, backed up by a gang. But even then, I doubt it. And you're soft now—" As he was speaking he saw Prior's expression change, and had time to wonder whether it was really wise to be taunting him. But the door was wide now, and Sir Nicholas stood there with old Mr. Mallory close behind him; and still there had been no sound.

"—no guts for anything but to shoot from ambush. You can't even do a job like this alone." It was all he could do not to follow uncle's movements in sheer fascination. Sir Nicholas reached behind him, and incredibly, unprompted, old Mr. Mallory put in his hand a bound copy of the Law Reports which lay on the table near the door; armed with this, counsel moved forward, still silently, still with his normal leisurely air, and holding the volume in both hands brought it down, hard, on the back of Prior's head. At the same instant Antony went over backward, as instinct dictated . . . a painful business, as instinct took no cognizance of the fact that he would land half across the fender, with one elbow in the coal scuttle. The gun went off harmlessly, and its owner lost, for the moment, all interest in the proceedings.

There was a silence. Then Sir Nicholas returned the book carefully to its place on the table and stooped to pick up the revolver. Mr. Mallory, after one dagger glance at Antony, started to pick his way across the room, his normal stateliness quite undisturbed by having to step across Stanley Prior's body to reach the desk. He already had his hand on the telephone when Antony succeeded in disentangling himself and scrambled to his feet. "Wait a bit," he said, urgently. "What are you going to do?"

"We should lose no time in communicating with the police."

"Well, don't. Not yet. There are things to settle first," he added to his uncle.

Sir Nicholas sighed. "I suppose you know your own business best," he remarked, and looked down, as though in surprise, at the revolver.

"It can't do any harm, just a few minutes' delay." Antony was moving his right arm experimentally, but if it pained him he made no mention of the fact. "I suppose you realize you saved my life," he said, at which Mr. Mallory looked wooden, and Sir Nicholas said bitterly: "I can't think why I bothered."

Antony raised an inquiring eyebrow. "What's up, sir?"

"Everything," said his uncle, comprehensively.

"But—"

"Sir Nicholas," said Mr. Mallory, in the tone of one whose patience is exhausted, "you can't mean to—to condone this violence."

"As the violence seems to have been rather one-sided—"

"It will look well in the headlines," said Antony, dreamily. " 'Queen's Counsel Fells Would-be Assassin.' Aided—of course — by heroic clerk," he added, not without malice.

Mr. Mallory compressed his lips and said stiffly, "I shall be in my own office, Sir Nicholas, if you need me." A moment later the door closed behind him with an exaggeration of gentleness.

"That's all very well," said Sir Nicholas. "I thought you wanted to catch this fellow Prior."

"I do. We have, haven't we? And what's more, sir, he's finished whatever swindle he was operating, so we can probably get Mrs. Edgecombe-Daly to charge him, too. But this other chap—"

Sir Nicholas looked at the recumbent figure of the burly man with revulsion. "Who is it?" he asked.

"Roberts. The other half of Sunday evening's act."

"And would it be indiscreet to inquire what you did to him?"

"Rough and ready methods, sir. You wouldn't approve. At least—"

"Is he all right?" asked Sir Nicholas, ignoring the implications of a doubtful look at Stanley Prior.

"Give him another ten minutes," said Antony.

"And you want to let him go? Why did he come here?"

"To kill me," said Antony; unreasonably, the statement sounded apologetic. "But you see, sir he hasn't hurt me, and—"

" 'I would have knocked the factious dogs on the head, to be sure, but I was not *vexed*,' " said Sir Nicholas. Antony grinned at him.

"I'd better explain," he said.

His uncle heard him in silence and nodded grimly when he finished with the assertion, "When he realizes half London knows what he's been up to, he won't try again."

"Probably not. I'll do as you ask, but I can tell you this, Antony: if I thought his purpose was merely to assault you I should be seriously tempted to give him every facility. And my blessing."

"What have I done now?"

"I should have known," said Sir Nicholas, gesturing in a distraught way with the hand that held the revolver, "that having invited your participation in Miss Wentworth's affairs I could expect nothing but confusion."

"I know Mallory thinks it's my fault those two chaps came here, but I didn't exactly invite them," Antony pointed out.

"I'm not complaining about that. I admit it is no more than I might have expected. What do I keep fire irons for if not to assault unwelcome visitors?"

"Or subscribe to the Law Reports," said Antony, unfairly. "But if you don't mind bodies on the floor and bullet holes in the paneling, what have I done to give you these uncharitable thoughts?" Sir Nicholas made no immediate reply, but his look was unmistakably reproachful, and his nephew added with an air of enlightenment, "I was afraid Barbara Wentworth would go to pieces when Lamb got at her."

"She made an excellent witness," said Sir Nicholas, obviously determined to give the devil his due. "She didn't lose her head *or* her temper, but, of course, she had nothing to say that was useful."

"You knew that already."

"I did. But perhaps I should explain to you that it is no longer my concern," said Sir Nicholas, carefully. "My only remaining duty to Miss Wentworth is to explain to the court tomorrow that the matter has been taken out of my hands—and Stringer's."

"Uncle Nick . . . you can't!"

"I have no choice. She refused categorically to allow us to call her niece. She said—" Sir Nicholas shuddered "—that if we did she'd stand up in the dock and confess to the whole thing."

"Then Derek was right. I was sure at this stage she'd agree."

"I thought so, too. Well, Bellerby explained the position to her, of course . . . but there was no need for quite such dramatic behavior. So then she told him to withdraw his instructions, a thing which has not happened to me," said Sir Nicholas, balefully, "in thirty years of practice."

Antony had been leaning against the corner of the desk. Now he stood up and said softly, "Obstinate, pugnacious . . . stubborn as a mule, you said, didn't you, Uncle Nick? But you can't help admiring her."

"*I* can."

"Well, if I can fix it . . . you wouldn't still back out, would you?"

"If my instructions are to continue—" He broke off and looked at his nephew helplessly. "You're right, of course, there is something admirable about the stand she's making. But why is she so determined—?"

"I can't stop to explain. I'll have to get hold of Bellerby and try to see her. Or should I send Derek?"

"His powers of persuasion seem no better than my own."

"This isn't persuasion . . . at least . . . more like obtaining cooperation with menaces," said Antony. "I say, sir, I think Prior's coming round. You know what to say to him, don't you?"

"I—er—may think of something," said Sir Nicholas, grimly.

"I meant, you'll have to keep him here till Roberts has gone . . . would you like me to . . . well, to make sure he won't come round too soon?"

"Certainly not. After all, I am armed. I may even discover an aptitude in myself for this sort of thing."

"Well, if you're sure." He paused in the doorway. "You could always call Mallory," he suggested.

Sir Nicholas relaxed suddenly and gave his nephew a companionable grin. "He'll never forgive either of us for this evening's work," he predicted. "When he remembers that he handed me that book—"

It was at this point that Antony realized his learned relative was enjoying himself, and that he could quite safely leave him to sort out the situation.

TWO HOURS LATER, in the interview room at the prison, Mr. Bellerby was listening without hope while Derek Stringer doggedly recapitulated the arguments his leader had used without effect earlier in the day. Barbara Wentworth heard him in silence, and then, "It's no use," she told him. "I meant what I said . . . I meant every word of it."

Mr. Bellerby thought wearily that now, perhaps, they could go home. He was as deeply concerned as ever for his client's affairs, but they seemed to have reached an impasse. But a moment later he was shocked out of his apathy.

Derek got up. He moved slowly but purposefully, as though he had given up the attempt to make her change her mind. "I thought you were fond of your niece," he said.

"Do you think I'm not?" At least he had shaken her out of that damned calm of hers. The green eyes blazed up at him.

"I'm beginning to wonder," he said deliberately and turned away.

"But . . . why? You can't leave it like that, you've got to tell me."

"What's the use?" But he swung round to face her again as he spoke, and leaned forward with his hands on the table. "If you want to be convicted, that's your lookout," he said, roughly. "Not even mine, though I happen to care what becomes of you. But you've no right to let them send Clare to an asylum, for want of the truth being told."

"She isn't mad!"

"But you won't be there to tell them that, will you?"

"I ... don't understand." She leaned forward suddenly, covering her face with her hands; it was the first crack he had seen in the hardness with which she had surrounded herself, and he had a sudden, horrible realization of what this trial had meant to her, of how much she had suffered every step of the way. More than even he had realized, though he had believed himself in sympathy with her. And more than ever today. He was appalled now by his own brutality and didn't realize that it was the only way he could have reached her.

He sat down again and said gently, "May I explain to you?" And she nodded her head in answer, but she did not lower her hands. Afterward he was to wonder whether he would ever have gained his point, if the events of day had not already bludgeoned her almost into a state of shock. But by that time the question was immaterial.

14

THERE WAS AN AIR of tension when the court assembled next morning. Sir Gerald was frankly bad-tempered, because he had sat up late the previous night, preparing his closing speech; and now here were two quite unforeseen witnesses, whose evidence would probably change the whole thing. His junior made a number of soothing remarks, which were not well received, and subsided into silence; he was not a man noted for his tact. As for the defense team, who had sat up equally late over their deliberations after Derek got back from Holloway, Stringer was heavy eyed, and seemed to have lost all his usual buoyancy; while his leader was speaking softly and generally radiating such an aura of sweetness and light that any sensible person who was able to do so would have kept well away. Behind them Mr. Bellerby sat, looking anxious, which would have further infuriated Sir Nicholas if he had turned round to look.

Before he came on to the bench Mr. Justice Carruthers had been wondering whether they were likely to finish that day, and if so, how late they would have to sit. He wasn't enjoying the case, because he would have liked to believe the prisoner innocent and found himself unable to do so. But, of course, the defense hadn't finished yet. He looked at Barbara Wentworth thoughtfully for a moment and then frowned a little, puzzled, because there was something different about her this morning, and he couldn't think what it was. After her long day in the witness box yesterday, she might have been expected to look haggard; perhaps her eyes were a little more shadowed than before, but apart from that she was just as startlingly lovely as ever. "For beauty lives with kindness," thought the judge, who had a streak of sentimentality that sometimes intruded itself at the most unexpected moments. At least it should in a well-ordered world. But what was different about her? It wasn't until he had let his mind and his eyes wander elsewhere that he realized that the carefully cultivated air of unconcern had deserted her. Up to now, whatever she had felt she wasn't showing; she might almost have been a statue for all the interest she displayed in what was going on. Perhaps with the end so near she was too tired to care any more that people should see her emotion; perhaps there was some other reason. Whatever it was, she was quiet and still as before, but her eyes betrayed her.

Before he had reached this conclusion, the judge had already noted that Maitland wasn't in court. Come to think of it, you'd have become giddy trying to keep track of his goings and comings this last week. But at this point the first witness claimed his attention, and he turned his head to watch Douglas Canning walk across to the witness box. Here was a man with his emotions held under the tightest rein. A tricky witness, thought Carruthers, not without sympathy for the defense counsel who would have to examine him; under considerable strain . . . you might get what you wanted out of him, and you might get something quite different. But that was Sir Nicholas's affair.

Outside, in the wide corridor, Clare Canning was sitting very upright on one of the long benches. Antony, moving a little stiffly this morning, as he did when he was tired or when his shoulder was paining him, came from the robing room and halted beside her. When she looked up to meet his eyes he thought she had a lost look; but then she said, "Good morning" primly and shifted her position a little—a token invitation only; there was already plenty of room.

He sat down and looked around him, and asked cautiously, "Is Emmie with you?"

"Daddy brought me. He's in there now—" Clare jerked her head in a gesture less ladylike than any he had so far seen from her "—and I think he asked the gentleman standing by the door to keep an eye on me, but of course I'm quite all right." She spoke firmly, but he thought it was for her own reassurance.

"Of course you are." He looked up and smiled at the uniformed attendant, who knew him well by sight and was looking at them indulgently.

"Emmie was upset," said Clare, confidentially. "Do you think it could still have been because Daddy was so cross the other evening?"

"Wednesday evening?" said Antony, feeling guilty.

"Yes, the day you came to see us. He shouted at her, and she cried." Antony said nothing, for the simple reason there seemed to be nothing he could say to that; Clare gave him a sidelong look, so that he wondered for a moment whether she could possibly be trying to embarrass him. "Afterward they pretended nothing had happened," she went on. "I wish I was grown up; then people would stop behaving as if I was blind, and dead, and *stupid*."

"We pretend for our own sakes, really." The remark had made him uneasy; it underlined too neatly what he was already feeling. She was altogether too clear-sighted, this child, and he was conscious of something very near to panic when he thought what they might be doing to her, between them. "You have to make allowances," he said.

"Do you shout when you're angry?" Just for the moment she had again the appraising look of an artist, and the question was obviously asked in a spirit of pure research.

"I don't know. I don't think so." It had never occurred to him to consider the question. But he couldn't leave her there, on this impersonal plane, he had to take her into a nightmare, grown-up world; and the only kindness he could do was not to minimize the step he was forcing her to take, not to say, or think, she's only a little girl, she'll soon forget. "Will you mind very much going in there and answering questions?"

"I don't know. Daddy said there's nothing to worry about."

"There isn't. I just thought you might find it a little strange."

"Will there be an awful lot of people?"

"Quite a lot. But you'll only have to talk to one or two of them, you know. There's the judge—"

"He'll be wearing a special fancy dress," said Clare, nodding. "I've seen pictures."

"That's right. Then my uncle—"

"Is he like you?"

"Not a bit." The likeness was one of expression only, and he was quite unconscious of it. "But he'll be dressed the same way. And so will some of the others, too."

"Why do you wear those things? Is it make-believe?"

"Not really." He paused, seeking for words. "Not pretending so much as remembering, Clare," he said; and saw her expression guarded and watchful suddenly. She wasn't listening to his careful explanation; she was lost in her own unhappy thoughts.

"Will they put me in prison if I don't answer all the questions?" she asked.

"No!" The answer came so explosively he was afraid he might have startled her.

"What will they do to me!"

"Nothing. Nothing at all. I promise. But, Clare—"

"Yes?" She was looking up at him trustingly, and now, disconcertingly, she tucked her hand in his.

"If you wanted to play a joke, and I promised to help you—"

"Do you think that's what it was . . . a joke?"

"It would have to be, wouldn't it? It isn't anything to worry about, just a silly mistake that you can put right." He took her other hand as he spoke, and both were as cold as ice; but he had the absurd feeling as they sat there that she wasn't a little girl anymore . . . not even his contemporary . . . but older, and a good deal wiser.

"When people are joking," he said, sadly, "their eyes look different . . . don't you think?" He didn't answer. He had forced her into the open now and she wouldn't accept the pitiful rags of self-deception he had offered her to cover the naked bones of truth. And he thought suddenly, I can give her nothing . . . it is I who am clinging to her for strength and reassurance.

But whichever of them was comforting the other, they sat like that in silence for a long time.

IN THE COURTROOM Sir Nicholas had finished his preliminary questions. "Now, will you tell us, Mr. Canning, when you last saw your former wife?"

"On the eighteenth of September. The day she died." (Sir Gerald Lamb looked up quickly, and Burns, his junior, wrote something on his pad.)

"At what time did you see her?"

"I went to the flat at nine-thirty, and left again about ten o'clock." The answers were coming readily enough, but there was a jerkiness about his speech that spoke of nervousness.

"How did you obtain admission?"

"I rang the bell." He was looking straight in front of him, his eyes fixed on some point well above counsel's head.

"And then? I am sorry, Mr. Canning, but we must have these details."

"My daughter came down and let me in."

"She is the only child of your marriage to the late Mrs. Laura Canning?"

"Yes ... Clare."

"How old is she?"

"She will be twelve in January."

"And where was she residing at the time of which we speak?"

"With her mother."

"So she came down to let you in. Please tell us what happened then."

"I went upstairs to see Laura. Clare went back to bed."

"She had got up to admit you?"

"Yes."

"Why did you go to see Mrs. Canning that particular evening?"

There was a long silence. Sir Nicholas showed no impatience, no anxiety; but the Solicitor-General cleared his throat noisily and then looked all round him in melancholy apology. And as he waited for the answer Derek Stringer's hands clenched together painfully; if Canning answered this ... would it even then be plain sailing? But they'd come to the point where he might well have recourse to evasion.

"I wanted to talk to her." But he couldn't leave it there. "I'd heard she was going to marry again."

"That was of some concern to you?"

"Of course it was. I didn't like what I'd heard of the man, and there was Clare to consider."

"You felt it was urgent, since you went to see Mrs. Canning while she was still convalescent?"

"Yes, I ... yes, of course. I thought perhaps ... well, if I'd left it any longer it mightn't have been any good, you see."

"You felt she might have committed herself to some course of action?"

"Yes."

"Had she in fact done so?"

"I ... think so."

"She told you she had agreed to marry Mr. Stanley Prior?"

"She ... yes, she did."

"He had asked her, and she had given him her answer?"

"That's right." If he would volunteer one thing, just one thing, thought Derek despairingly, we might have a chance of getting somewhere. But if Sir Nicholas was becoming impatient, he gave no sign. He retraced his steps resignedly and started for his objective by another path.

"You have told us your daughter let you in, and then went back to bed. Was she in her night attire?"

"Yes, and it was cold on the staircase. I . . . we ran upstairs, to make her warm again."

"And she retired immediately?"

"She went to her room."

"And you went in to talk to your wife?"

"To Laura . . . yes."

"Was she in good spirits?"

"Well . . . . "

"Was she cheerful? Depressed?"

"She was . . . well, she didn't like me coming, you see."

"Why was that, Mr. Canning?"

"Well, she *said* it was inconsiderate . . . she was ill, and Clare would have caught cold, going downstairs in her bare feet."

"Do I understand you correctly? She said that, but she meant something else?"

"I had a right to see Clare sometimes. But Laura didn't like it."

"This would not be her only emotion, however . . . this rather querulous dislike of your visit?"

"No. I'd say she was just as usual."

"Cheerful?"

"She wasn't ever really hilarious."

"Then . . . in low spirits?"

"Not that, either. Well . . . not at first."

"She became depressed in the course of your visit?" Perhaps only Derek noticed the slight relaxation in his leader's attitude, the faint note of relief that crept into his voice. He wasn't going to get any help from Canning, he hadn't expected to. But that was the first slip . . . the first sign that they might—at last—be getting somewhere.

"Well . . . yes."

"In consequence of what you said to her?"

"I suppose so."

"If you don't know, Mr. Canning, perhaps you will give us the opportunity of judging for ourselves. What did you tell her?"

"That I didn't like the idea of Prior being Clare's stepfather. She said it was nothing to do with me."

"Had you expected to be able to influence her?"

"No, I . . . I thought perhaps she might agree, after all, that Clare could come to me."

"Did she agree to that?"

"She just laughed . . . she said she wasn't such an unnatural mother. So I told her," said Douglas, grimly, "a thing or two about this chap—"

"Ah, yes. You had your own reasons for disapproving of Mr. Prior's suit. I'm afraid we mustn't go into them now."

"No . . . well, I don't want to 'go into' anything," the witness pointed out.

"But I must trespass on your patience a little longer. Did this information have any influence at all on Mrs. Canning's intentions?"

"I couldn't prove anything, you see. It was just hearsay."

The judge looked up. "Does that mean no, Mr. Canning?" he wondered.

"Yes, my lord."

"I am obliged to you." Carruthers made a note.

"You left Mrs. Canning, you tell us, at about ten o'clock," said Sir Nicholas.

The witness looked puzzled. "Yes, I did."

"And did you meet somebody in the street as you were leaving?"

"Miss Wentworth."

"Please describe this meeting."

"A car was driving away. She seemed to be staring after it. Then she turned and saw me." And now for the first time he looked across at the still figure in the dock. "We talked," he said. "We talked for about a quarter of an hour." He was staring at Barbara now, and just for a moment she looked back at him, her face almost expressionless; then her eyes dropped, and Douglas turned away and said, as though in despair, "So she didn't go in till a quarter past ten. And I went home."

"What did you talk about, all that time?"

"Well . . . Clare."

"All the time?"

"I think so. I don't really remember."

"Your mind did not go back to this conversation the next day . . . when you heard what had happened . . . when you knew your sister-in-law had been arrested?"